Praise for the books of
Stephan Jaramillo

Chocolate Jesus

"Stephan Jaramillo has created a wild romp through America's fast-food culture. His cast of comically flawed characters is flawlessly drawn, and his sense of social satire is as smooth and sweet as—well—chocolate." —Christopher Moore,
author of *Island of the Sequined Love Nun*

"[An] oddball protagonist . . . The book's over-the-top quality is fun . . ." —*New York Times Book Review*

"Amusing . . . Jaramillo has an endearing sympathy for his goofy characters." —*Publishers Weekly*

Going Postal

"A hilarious first novel." —*Details*

"Jaramillo capture[s] the mindset of the quintessential slacker." —*New York Times Book Review*

"Surprisingly uplifting . . . delightfully optimistic . . . ultimately life-affirming and a pleasure to read." —*Swing*

"Judging from *Going Postal*, Stephan Jaramillo has a true comic gift, and absolutely no business being armed." —Sherwood Kiraly,
author of *Who's Hot/Who's Not*

Continued . . .

the scoundrel

stephan jaramillo

BERKLEY BOOKS, NEW YORK

Credit for the E-mails belongs to Dan Cummings.

This book is an original publication of The Berkley Publishing Group.

THE SCOUNDREL

A Berkley Book / published by arrangement with
the author

PRINTING HISTORY
Berkley trade paperback edition / May 1999

The Penguin Putnam Inc. World Wide Web site address is
http://www.penguinputnam.com

ISBN: 0-425-16859-X

I'd like to thank all those people who believed and whose support (emotional, physical and fermented) made this possible. You know who you are: Danny (who I want to say never had a job where he had to wear a rabbit costume), Stacy (who was there Day One, Ground Zero—you're the best), Benjie, Anna, Gilda, Richard, Lisa, Steve B., Tony, et al.

I'd also like to thank Lisa Considine, my editor, and Thomas Cherwin, my copyeditor, for an excellent job.

And thanks to Jimmy Vines, my agent for his support in my literary vision, if one exists.

And I especially want to thank Gary Goldstein for finding my work in the slush pile to begin with. If it wasn't for him I'd still be working in a restaurant. Oh, I still am. Well, thanks a million anyway.

the scoundrel

prologue

It was the year Time didn't move quite right. The year the Forces of Nature were all out of sorts. The year the big rains came. The year I couldn't quite get a grip when I was in the midst. It was the year of El Niño and nothing was as it should be. It was the year . . . She left.

Until then it seemed life always puttered along in obscure fits and tepid slipstreams, in vague marches or oblivion-destinated excess. Life flew down a stream of chaotic real time (revealed later to be crystalline in the exactness of its structure). It glided with and struggled against the various competing currents.

I was able to measure and mark this life of mine with women, jobs, professional sports playoffs, the release of seasonal microbrewed beers and the harvest of Northern Cali green bud. Nothing too spectacular. I had no Year the Car Fell on My Face. The Fall I Became President. My First Prime Time Sitcom. Nothing like that. My life was marked by: Getting fired on the Fourth of July. The girl I had in an Amtrak train bathroom. The trip to Reno when Mike and I won four hundred bucks. That time my girlfriend began fucking an acquaintance (I didn't even have the "girlfriend fucks best friend" one). The Giants winning the Super Bowl. The five years at Saxon's Restaurant.

1997 was different. 1997 was a gibberish. A cacophonic mess of delight, perplexity and pain. The agony and the ecstasy. It made no sense. All was topsy-turvy. Fast and slow, hot and cold. It was the year time cracked. The year . . . She left.

And it all began just fuckin'

Boom!

It's 1997 and

Boom!

My little world was shattered.

Let me tell you how it went. This is how it went. January 5th I believe it was (actually, the date is branded in my mind, the exact moment, every twist and turn of that endless night's darkness, but even here, on the page, two years later, I still must pretend a certain indifference). I had just returned from Mexico, another dip down south to refuel my psyche and gain strength for another ten to sixteen months of a job that would grind me down and require me to again step away and refuel.

I missed her, of course. I always missed her most when I was far away and I wanted her most on the eve of reunion and sipping my endless free international flight drink (it seems that Jack y Coke in Spanish gets you a plastic cup filled with eight ounces of each on Aeromexico Flight #388) I let go of all our little tiffs and petty squabbles and the strife that had come to near dominate the past six months living together. I forgot the three or four times we'd reluctantly come to the conclusion that it just wasn't a go. That we couldn't make it work out. I stepped off the plane enthusiastic.

But instead of great embrace and joy for a new year, on January 5th I could hardly sleep. It was the longest night of my fucking life ("I'm moving out" ran again and again through my brain all night long. They looped it, they looped it). The darkness was formidable and defiant a fortnight from the solstice and I thought night might never end lying there in what had been our bed but what was now transformed into some sick-fuck Mr. Toad's Wild Pirates of the Brokenhearted Caribbean ride. Oh God, my mind races, will hot fine lovelies fuck me?—"I'm moving out," her voice keeps saying—or will I live forever wanting her back—"I'm moving out"—ruing my foolish folly in letting this gem slip through my fingers, fuck her, fuck her. I then shiver in fear for my life.

But the next day, January 6th, somehow arrives, the sun somehow rises despite my crisis and I go and ring up my best buddy—all I had—and there he was saying, come on down to the pub, we'll watch the game. It was a Niners-Packers play-off.

"I don't see why you give a shit. That's your problem." Mike, my best buddy in the whole wide world is telling me this at Jacko's, sometimes upstairs, sometimes down. We don't give a shit. The game warbles lamely in the background. "You said it wasn't working."

"Yeah, I know. . . ." I knew he was right. That I just shouldn't care, that it hadn't been working. I knew what he was getting at. In a way. Translate my suddenly single life entirely into monetary expenditure and genital fulfillment currency and forget all the emotional claptrap. That's for the girls to sweat. But I was a sucker for love, especially fresh from a loss. I couldn't hardly help myself even if love really did suck the day after . . . She left. . . . She swings an arm and dashes to bits my masculinity, letting out her woeful bitch yell,

AIYEEEHH!! AIYEEEHH!!

"If you don't give a shit you get a lot further." Mike looked at me very seriously and since he was my best friend and had been single for most of the years . . . She and I were together and he did have at least three or four stories involving chicks who fuck (you didn't want to do the math, it came out to one every four months or so) he had some cred and sometimes, when you're talkin' smack with the boys late at night, the idea of not giving a shit sounds really really good and the woman asleep upstairs in your bedroom loses her warmth and you forget the warm baked comfort that emanates when you open the bedroom door. Instead she takes on the mass of an anchor. Dead weight holding you down. And now that I didn't even have such an anchor (my suddenly single heart quivered in some dark recess of my soul and I was lost removed from the women womb source sweet pussy love embrace) I decided that night to be just like Mike. To forget caring. Forget love. To now join him in his single freedom and together we'd realize sexual conquests that would have had Alexander the Great jealous had he been a pussy hound instead of a world conqueror. Mike and I were gonna score.

So "Fuck Love" became my basic philosophy of life for that El Niño year that began with my woman leaving. Post-January 6th, my plan was to go around thinking, "Fuck Love!" I would resurrect my being in the guise of the great Antimonogamist and in some devil-may-care mayhem leave a Sherman's March to the Sea-sized swath of broken hearts and quivering loins in my wake.

the gatekeeper

At long last the walls have been scaled, the defenses breached, a beachhead established. Entrance into the fortress is finally mine. It is 9:17 on a Wednesday night, October eighth, and after two months, —twenty-three days and eighty-four nights—I once again find myself in the confines of a single woman's apartment.

Mmmm, her very essence hangs about the place in the cigarette-stale smoke and doggy-scented air of her bedroom and I breathe deeply of it. That distinct smell of another and since it's the scent of a woman (the "girliness" of it, that wonderful "girliness" after all the coarse manly rooms I'd been exiled to) it excites me.

It really is a strange animal's lair. There lies the bed she sleeps in, her body's perfume infused into its sheets. A closed novel sits on the tiny table next to her bed with an empty coffee mug and an ashtray filled with strange foreign cigarette butts and then there are all those things soft and cute which many women specialize in, though this woman's room was marine barracks spartan.

"Would you like some tea?" she asked when we first stepped inside ("Vud jew lie ache," it sounded like). She's Russian which in these post-Cold War New Millennium Days is now juicy as shit. Her accent is impossibly erotic. All of my friends want to sleep with former Soviet bloc women: Czechs, Romanians. God, how I craved a Hungarian girl with hair as black as obsidian.

I remembered back to when "The Women of the Eastern Bloc" was a photo spread that might have bankrupted *Playboy*. Masculine steroid-whacked swimmers with shoulders like a young Burt Lancaster in *Crimson Pirate*, Santa Claus-waisted Stroganoff-slurping peasant babushkas, dull-looking steppebillies with thick Evolution Lite facial features. Who would want to fuck a Russian back then? Not even considering the political ramifications.

But now? My kingdom for a five-foot-eleven Slovak beauty. A fine-boned Latvian. Just think of those mail-order Ukrainians! And me, here, tonight, sitting in the bedroom of an authentic Muscovite. If I can ever crack her code I'll feel that some sort of Patriotic Duty has been fulfilled (The President walks up shaking the hands of all the Nation's Heroes. "And what did you do for your country, my fellow American?" "Well, I fucked this chick from Moscow, Mr. President." "Keep up the good work, son," he says as I bow to receive my medal).

Forget American women. With them I gotta know shit about the Brady Bunch and answer questions about my economic condition as if they were eager young IRS agents. No, let me fall into the arms of this Russian woman with her downturned mouth of thin lips save for the ripe pout in the center of her lower. Her steely blue gray eyes. Their color is dead-of-winter icy and I imagine the ones she must have seen.

"Would you like sugar in your tea?" she asked as she peeked her head in the doorway adjoining the bedroom to the shared kitchen.

"Sure," I said with a grand smile. It came out far too cheerful. Be careful, I told myself, they can smell eagerness. Don't even mentally visualize the word "desperate" or think in any way about your dick. They'll know. Even if they are Russian and there's a slight language barrier.

We're at the predating stage here. This is the courtship dance and you have to start out as though sex is the furthest thing from anybody's mind. If there's to be any de-pantsing of them in the future you have to act as if the idea of de-pansting anyone rarely occurs to you.

But I was difficult to resist my amazement. It had been so long since I'd had my hands on the warm soft flesh of a woman and here I was inches away from a young woman's bed. I wanted to bury my face in her pillow and revel in her hair's bouquet. I had not hardly touched a woman except for a couple of stray family and female coworker hugs in the past six fortnights. At times the fact of that fast of flesh could overwhelm me.

But everything comes and goes. All in its time. Every dog has its day. Something about seasons. There's plenty of aphoristic evidence to support my hope that . . . yes, the worm had turned and here I was in the intimate realms of a Russian woman's apartment on Derby, just south of campus.

Things were looking good. I surveyed the room, examined her secret animal den as she rummaged about in the yellow light of the kitchen. She had so many books, this girl. I smiled as I admired the sheer intellectual bravado of her book collection. She was a heavyweight. Capote, Brodsky, writers with Russian names I didn't recognize and odd-looking boxes of Russian cigarettes that her mother sent her from the Motherland.

Her furniture consisted of a desk, the tiny table, the bed and a "love" seat which my ass is parked on. It's perfect. She had virtually nowhere to sit except for near me. Not only that, but I'm in possession of a manuscript, which was what first excited her former-communist blood.

I had met . . . let's call her Anastasia. It's a favorite childhood movie of mine starring one of my three great screen loves, Ingrid Bergman. It was 1956 and Ingrid was as vulnerable and beautiful as ever. But I was at a cafe and not trying to fool any Dowager Empresses.

It always happens at a cafe. I had a pile of papers sitting in front of me when "Anastasia" first walked up. She looked sullen, the corners of her mouth turned down, her eyes a clear and neutral blue-gray.

"Vell, can I use your sugar?" began our exchange.

Anastasia walked in from the kitchen carrying two steaming cups of tea and I began to get excited and allowed myself to celebrate the possible end of my long, long drought. The time had finally come. The touchless, fleshless, loveless, sexless days and, more importantly, nights had at long last come to an end. Would she take the bed or come and sit next to me here on the "love" seat?

SHAPAFF!!

Anastasia produced, out of seemingly thin air, a hard-backed wooden chair as though she'd studied under David Copperfield.

Where the hell did *that* come from? I wondered as I took the saucer and cup she offered me. That chair was *nowhere!* a minute ago. It must have come out of her pants pocket. It was one of those school punishment chairs, extra stiff and hard with the strategically designed back that digs into your spine after a few minutes.

Anastasia neatly placed the chair 132 cms away from me (so that if I stretched my entire body and reached with my toes without actually sliding down from the not even "love" seat I would still be approximately one penis length away from her). Suddenly my sky darkened and I felt winter's tug.

"How is your tea?" she asked sincerely.

"Mmm, good." In real life I'm a coffee drinker. "Haven't had tea in a long time." I smiled. There was just no way to get at her. I might as well have been sitting out in the hallway. My Russian Love out there in the middle of the now huge room, in the middle of that bare hardwood floor, her beautiful Slavic bottom (and this woman had a bum on her that will forever make me angrily scoff at the propaganda my government once fed me) parked on that hardwood chair and me alone over here amidst the warm lights and soft cushions.

But nine months of being single had seasoned me. I was experienced enough now to not panic and lose my head. I sit through a two-hour intellectual conversation (during which she detailed for me the difference between the melancholic and phlegmatic personality), the cup of tea, the smoking of what she called a "Russian joint," and decided to try again another night when the forces might be in my favor.

I took my leave and a foggy cold walk home, but not before taking her hand and giving her a soft kiss on her Russian Jewish lips. She was neither eager nor actively resistant. I imagined that her father once treated questions from the Secret Police in a similar manner. I promise to call her and on the walk home plotted the strategy to gain her moist nether regions.

the days of maria cordova

I walked home from the Russian woman's house, past the video store. It's closed. I can't even rent a movie and so in the cool October night air, after dreaming on Anastasia for a bit I thought about . . . Her for a second. The time we practically ran into each other rounding a corner in the house. She was coming out of the bathroom, her dark hair jet black from the wetness. Her dark beauty knocked me back more than the surprise. But ten months later that kind of thinking doesn't sit too well as I'm heading to an empty bed so I thought back to this other girl who's more fun to think about.

It was right after . . . She left and life was the most miserable thing. Women nearly recoiled from me and I began to crawl into myself despite my vow of amazing singledom. Mike's turned over his genitals to Kat, he's a married man now and then comes February, a famously cold and cruel month, when the sun hangs sickly in the Aquarian sky and I'm sad and broken as can be. No women in the known world will have me. I'm convinced they can smell the loss and broken nature of my self. What a troll I am.

But thankfully along comes a girl to save me. Just for a minute like they sometimes will. Maria Cordova. Maria became, quickly and forcefully, a part of . . . Her.

I had bought a computer because I'd finally been led to believe that life was simply impossible without one (not to mention that I reached the point where I simply couldn't, not even one more time, tell someone that I didn't have an E-mail address only to see their face fall and then be given a lecture if not treated to some outright derision).

So I plugged it in and powered it up and within four minutes of being on the Internet I was looking for sex. Not the fake kind or the pictures, though I looked at those, too, but the real kind. Real people who, hopefully, really were the hot women they claimed to be.

There was a lot of typing and waiting and getting nothing, no response (same as the real world, but my rejection is now in the privacy of my own home and therefore counts somehow for less), but soon I had a live one on the line.

Maria Cordova lived in San Jose and—if her first messages were to be believed—was the hottest piece of ass around.

Well, let's see, I'm working on the "perfect body." The men in my office love me in the summer, I don't wear any panty hose with my (short) skirts to work and my tan legs really do something.

Oh, yeah they do and so does that (short) wrapped in that tight little parenthetical. Oh, man. I shoulda got a computer a long time ago but then I thought about . . . Her (. . . dead silence). K—— wouldn'ta liked that too much. I smile at the thought. This is what I'm after. Fuck love, I just want a hottie.

The very next day she's back with another E-mail. It has some words about her interests, a sentence about her background and she might have even mentioned some job but it was *this* paragraph that caught my attention:

> I'm very lean and since I'm petite 5'3" 117 lbs I tend to look better in less clothes than most petite women. Everyone tells me I have "sex appeal." My girlfriends tell me I have a nice a** for tong underwear. They tell me I should be a Victoria's Secret model.

Tongs, thongs, whatever. Either way this is exactly what I've been looking for. This is exactly what I needed to start my great year. A hot chick who only seems to be interested in sex. On a computer no less! I was enamored with technology that month.

But there's something virtual and unreal about it and I scratch my head and search the back of the computer making sure all the wires and plugs seem right. They're fine. Hmmm, I give her my phone number, cross my fingers and hope for the best.

In a couple of days I receive an E-mail that has me reaching down inadvertently to my package to properly position it for the rest of her letter.

> Thanks for the phone number. I'm gonna call. Are you ready? Let's see you know everything, my legs, my boobs (I'm 36c-23-34 How's that?!?!), my waist is tiny my stomach is very flat and my hips are, well nice, and of course we runners tend to have a nice firm ass . . . How's that?!?! I have brown eyes, full lips, long brown hair, firm arms, well I guess the picture is complete. . . . Hope I painted a vivid picture?!?!
> I'll call you tomorrow, maybe we can get together this weekend.

I stare at the computer screen dumbfounded. It sounds too hot to be true. She's telling me about her ass, her tits. It's gotta be fake. It's some *guy!*

"It's a dude!!" my brain screams and I drop "it" in a flash and reach for the power button.

But then I look at the calendar. February 8. Of course! If she's actually a woman, she's high as a kite on pre-Valentine's hype. For once maybe I might use Valentine's Day for my very own evil purposes (though I don't really think my purposes are evil—they just kinda sound like it a little bit now and then).

I felt a little funny having "busted" myself masturbating to the computer earlier in the week, but it was all for naught because the day of the meeting takes place. I'm in North Beach on the lookout for a supposedly hot Latina (possibly TS, I'm full-on red radar alert for TVs, TSs . . . any sort of T activity and I'm gone).

But there she was and looking back the thing I'll never understand about Maria Cordova was why the fuck she ever fucked me in the first place but I thanked the gods that she fuckin' did.

We met in North Beach at some crappy ass restaurant. It was gonna be her and another couple, friends of hers. I'm about to meet my very first cyberpal.

She was leaning against the wall in front of the place the third time I passed by (after asking the maître d' twice about the arrival of my "friends" that was now out), one foot against the wall wearing this short skirt and heels, no stockings (just like she said!). Her legs were amazing and her skin a perfect natural tan. Long black hair, a pert little nose, the dark wet eyes, a perfect Latina and best of all, not even a man after all. No, Maria Cordova was all woman. The kind of girl a guy could lose himself in.

We said hello in that nervous first-meeting air. She gave me a warm hug and then a couple of more. I nuzzled her neck a bit and she seemed to like this.

"My friends are trying to find parking. They should be here pretty soon," she told me. "So, what do you think?"

She displayed her self as though she was familiar with how most men sized up women.

I smiled and pulled her toward me for another embrace. "You're very attractive," I spoke into her ear.

"Oh! There they are." she pulled away and began to wave at her friends in this happy-smiley face way that kind of bugged me.

Her friends were from the Silicon Tribe, which was a notoriously bad match for the Berkeley Tribe. Her girlfriend had that facial soap commercial actress look about her while the man—the very pink man—personified the profile I had worked up in my Berkeley living room on Silicon Valley hi-tech types: a neat and clean orderly moneyed suspicious isolationist all-American frat boy type who might be nice no doubt, but who you knew was adept at pasting on fake smiles of goodwill so you're never quite sure where you really stand. His jeans had that too perfect fade to them and his shirts, like his views on the world, were tucked in a little too tight and he wore white tennies completely spotless and drove a BMW which he pooh-poohed as just a car (they wanted to take mine and the blood either drained or rushed to my face at the thought; I can't remember. My wrecky van that hovered between homeless hippie and serial killer. It had taken on a life of its own and would soon be put out of its misery after a few more hundred dollars' worth of repairs. The very idea of them even setting eyes on my car immediately put in my mind's eye the now realized fully luscious Maria Cordova on a boat fading into the distance of a transatlantic voyage waving good-bye forever).

Thankfully we took the BMW and Maria and I are in the dark backseat. I was buzzing from the close distance of the worlds in that tiny backseat they put in BMW 320i's. It was kinda cool hanging for a moment with these Silicon Valley natives who spoke of computers as God and stocks and status as a Religion. Money was their mania. They quickly convinced me of their wealth, but somehow I'm dishing out for everything. Caught up in her game, I immediately knew that I was to pay. That was a man's role she took as nonnegotiable. I'd forgotten that dating costs a little more than sitting on the couch, the two of us with burritos watching *Seinfeld,* but I gladly obliged. I mean, her body!

We go to Johnny Love's (a place I would never go myself and had never been before and have never been since, but aspiring to be a good scoundrel hot on the scent they could have dragged me to the lame, the boring, the overpriced, the dangerous, even the misdemeanor illegal in my hope for the pussy. I'm dumb as a blood-hound at times, but you'd forgive me this time for the girl was goddess-created).

We get up to dance and make our way through the jam of people. It's shoulder-to-shoulder in most spots with the guys clutching their bottles of beer close to their sides and the women with their cocktails poised above their shoulders, and, thankfully, the dance floor was so completely packed that there was very little room for any sort of movement of any kind which suited to a T my style of dancing. The beyond-fire-marshal density on the dance floor that night highlighted all that was best about my dance moves: my nodding head and smiling groove to the beat. The gods smiled high from above.

So I've got my hands on her amazing hips. Her entire body is as smooth and firm and fine as I'd ever had my hands on and she's smiling that fuck-me/not-yet look and we get off the floor and take a break off to the side and she's letting me handle quite a bit considering that we've just met and the place is as public as it can get, but this only encourages me.

We're kissing and she kisses pretty good and then she kisses even better and we keep breaking and I look around sheepishly and then go in for some more and draw the line at her breasts because I'm looking for more being the more mature and responsible long-view kind of guy nowadays in all facets of my life. Ever since . . . She left I'm on a whole new program.

We head back to the table and I've got this fine young Latina in my arms and she's a knockout. She's got all sorts of guys checkin' her out. I can see the eyes turn toward her as she marches fearlessly through the crowd. The men look at her as she goes by and I take the opportunity to look at them smiling like I got a handle on this shit that you can't believe, far beyond the reality, but the reality for them was in my look as I stroked her hips nodding to one guy we walked past like, Brotha I got the shit tonight let us all celebrate as Men with a capital M.

Back at the table are her friends who I can't quite figure. They weren't doin' it—the girl had some multimillionaire boyfriend who didn't spend much time with her but was in on the chip or something, some ground zero computer net man from the Peninsula. They slip into their South Bay dialect of technojargon and Wall Streetese, so I occupy myself with stroking Maria's amazingly firm leg.

Though that was not his name I want to call him Bif and so I shall. Bif asked me man to man when the girls went to the bathroom,

"How's it going?" I remember him licking his lips though he didn't. I smiled and nodded and shrugged like I couldn't believe fucking any of this at all. Because I couldn't.

All I could think was that this was some sort of miracle delivered to me through my computer.

Zeus.com has spoken.

Sometime after the second Calistoga (they drank absolutely no alcohol; they were so healthy it was making me sick. Like they didn't even sweat—"Their shit doesn't stink," my old man would say) and before the cleanup (when I was told finally that my entire face was smeared with lipstick. They all had a laugh and I guess it was kinda stupid but I wore my Cover Girl as a badge that night) I decided—or more accurately, the moment of most concentrated clarity came upon me, and I saw that some god or force or energy or destiny or being, something, anything, but something greater than I was in effect, and that it had come to me through the use of the computer. The Internet was my oracle and I called it Zeus.com and it handed to me that night so close to Valentine's Day a girl in the form that I might have dreamt as some sort of heartrending ideal, but one I would never know. But the gods were bored or one had lost a bet and so they tugged at the strings through the cosmos and tossed into my lap Maria Cordova and in the very midst of becoming a heartbreaker hot chick fucker I could feel myself falling for her.

the second night of maria cordova

During the high time of Maria Cordova, the peak of our season together (all two actual meetings, though the E-mails stretched it out over a month), I was a fucking hero. . . . She was knocked right out of the fucking park. Gone. Good riddance. 'Cause one look at Maria Cordova and her firm fat-free but nevertheless voluptuousness and I was gone. I'd catch myself with a dazed grin staring out the window dreaming about . . . her. Maria. What was I thinking?

But a week after our first meeting I'm driving south past Fremont and Hayward (I can never remember which comes second—is it San Lorenzo or Leandro? I don't know) where the South Bay widens and flattens and turns gray and nondescript. Past all that was once orchards down the way to San Jose.

I had a rental car because while mine could nearly be trusted to make the trip I didn't want it seen in broad daylight (to this day she's the one girl I lost because of my wheels) and at last I pulled off the freeway into a near barrio. Always with the body shops and the taquería whose neon and hand-painted signs made me wonder what they might serve. I imagined it hot and spicy good and this made me think of the girl, Maria, in the same terms, as though her sexuality and cuisine were derived of the same roots and through her would come alive my own Latino roots. My Carrasco blood. I dreamed a nighttime stroll to the taquería with her on my arm, my newfound girl, to get spicier-than-shit tacos.

I pulled up to her house, which sat on a nondescript street of modest older two- and three-bedroom homes, a far cry from the extreme wealth and BMW prosperity she portrayed to me that night in San Francisco. But it wasn't her bank account that I was hoping to get a peek at.

She opened the door greeting me with a big smile, looking as cute as I'd remembered. I had my arms full of cooking gear and ingredients. I was employing my tried-and-true cooking seduction. It's the greatest setup. The woman is usually quite impressed, you're at a home (which means you have ready access to and will soon be innocently enough perched on a couch, a piece of furniture I almost require for my love life) and food is involved, which, for all but the most asleep utilitarian of eaters, is loaded with sensuality.

I've decided that the way to a woman's panties is through her stomach. Where our mothers and grandies seduced their men or closed the deal by the quality of their dinner fare, today there's hardly a woman whipping up a goddamned thing. You're supposed to take them out to dinner. The very idea of wistfully wishing for the feminine nurturing of a hot satisfying stew on a cold November evening smacks of feminism bashing or Neanderthal sociopolitics.

But I've turned the tables on them. Rather than take up the argument I've manned the kitchen in an end-around sweep that I'm hoping will take me into my red zone offense. I mostly rely on a warm zabaiglione for the clincher. That last course being of utmost importance, sitting on the couch, the wine should be mostly gone. We'll be eating something sweet. By then things'll have gotten dreamy as the night progresses . . .

But Maria Cordova, whose daddy loved his arroz con leche from his famed Guadalajara, didn't drink wine, and it didn't really matter in the end. Somehow about ninety seconds after my bringing in the last of it from the car and settling onto her couch (she was on the phone being rude I thought after a while) Maria was straddling me, leaning down for a kiss. It was good and warm and I accepted this as carte blanche as far as the fondling of every square inch of her entire body, over the clothes, and after the second kiss— she kept having to break away to get back to the conversation—I was even under the sweatery blouse and sizing up nicely her meaty breasts. It's flesh, baby!

Maria Cordova had come packed into a pair of Levi's that her Silicon Valley worship tried to negate, but her perfect round ass returned to the denim its usual life and spark. She seemed all so clean, so very neat in the tight pants and tight blouse, but she had all the curves in all the right places and you couldn't help but think about all the moist and hot underneath.

We break and she continues with the phone and goes on and on. She had me sitting there just watching her talk on the phone like it was surely more important than . . . me.

I took advantage to enjoy one of my favorite pastimes, the close examination of a woman's home. I look about and see again the Stephen King—it's nearly as common as a TV—and books about scary horror ghouly crap and pictures of her family (when Maria saw me looking at the family portrait of the sisters in their early twenties and late teens, she broke from the phone for a minute to challenge, "Who's the prettiest one? Huh!?").

She had to take a shower after six hours on the phone and I start the meal, low-fat and vegetarian which will go well with her dietary requirements. Pasta, which all the long-distance runners crave, in a style fitting to the entire affair: puttanesca.

It's the sauce of the whores of Napoli, so the story goes. It was piquant and aromatic and the rich tomato caper black olive smells would lure the men into the brothels—the best sauce being nearly as important as the lineup of girls.

The sauce has been made (it fuckin' rocks!) and it's simmering gently and the expensive Italian pasta, the four-buck-a-pound shit, is out and I drop it into the simmering water right when she comes out of the shower and calls to me. So I walk over to the bedroom and there she is in these thong panties (just as she often promised in her E-mails!) of the slickest silk and wickedest cut. Her ass is an engineering feat of magic. It hangs there as though gravity-defiant. My hands are drawn to her body like magnets. Her skin is a soft wonderful sensation. I pull her toward me and she smells so fresh out of the shower.

It was like some sort of joke and of course it could be no other than Zeus.com shining down upon me and there's no sense resisting the bed right there as she buries her tongue in my mouth as if for dear life. We're horizontal and in about 180 seconds I've slid her panties off and I'm down there on her tasty tight little brown Mexican box and it was bueno. Muy bueno.

Now I'm running back and forth from her bedroom to the kitchen. Going down on her, running into the kitchen to turn down the sauce, running back to the bedroom. She takes me in her mouth and after just loving it and looking her over like wonder candy I can't take any more, not another plunge of her mouth, so I pull away, back to the kitchen I go to stir the pasta in the finally roiling salted water, run back to the bedroom and slide on a condom like I'm Billy the Fucking Kid of Safe Sex.

Fwoop!

That thing's on to the root and I home in thinking, I should've brought penne, it takes longer to cook. I still got ten, twelve minutes.

And so of course after all that hot ass shit I'm sent home (after a second session; boy, I wanted my fill. I wanted to wash . . . Her away in a fuck of monumental proportions). I can't even spend the night—Maria Cordova will have none of that. I'm sent away to drive the forty-five miles back home at 11:45 at night instead of getting to spend the night in her wonderful bed.

I drive home and within seven miles down the road I think I'm madly in love with this woman who's arrived out of nowhere. Despite her wrong clothes, her wrong goals, her different values, despite my vow to have nothing to do with love. Despite the fact that she obviously just wants a fuck (and supposedly that's all I want), I easily deny it all and instead imagine that this is the girl to make me forget all about . . . Her.

But in the end Maria Cordova was a wicked joke. A double face smack. Back to back. January. February.

Smack! Smack-Smack!

I was veritably love-smote down.

Fuck.

work

Luckily it was time for another day of work and I stepped through the back door and into the kitchen in the early morning. When I work lunch I'm always the first one there, the kitchen's warm and comfy, it's quiet and peaceful as I fire up the espresso machine and try not to think of anything. It's the best thing about work; it takes my mind off. My existence shrinks down a bit which is nice.

As the espresso machine fired up I became a little perturbed by Anastasia's reluctance as well as the direction my "love life" was heading. My New Year's resolution to transform myself into a swinging sex stud who could cavalierly crumple the many phone numbers handed to me by young beauties if they didn't quite measure up . . . well, anyway.

And then there was my career. It wasn't exactly a career in the traditional sense as all planned out, but it was getting to the point where, by sheer weight of years, it had earned the title nonetheless. I had a common-law sort of career. And the problem I was having with this career was that I was downsizing not only in the size and reputation of the restaurants I worked at but also in the numbers of waitresses they employed. That was the main problem I had with working at Marco's. There are only three of them. I kept hoping a new one might be hired whom I could love.

Then the coffee came out of the machine and into my cup and I warmed some milk for it in a small saucepan and fired up the ovens and turned on the hoods anyway, ignoring the millionth urge to just quit and lead an exciting sex-filled vagabondian sort of existence.

That WHOOMPH! as the gas catches and the warm milk pours into my cup and the at-first loud and then silent white noise hum of the hood fans means the day has begun.

I work at a small Italian restaurant down in Oakland at the far end of a fancy avenue of fancy stores selling fancy coffee and fancy cigars, imported goodies at the Ultra Deli, rarefied supermarkets with carefully stocked items from England, Italy and France. Where people who pull up in Mercedes and BMWs and Lexi buy sugar in a box with a parrot on it, light brown sugar lumps that cost four or five bucks a pound and it phases them not.

But down on our end of the block, past the Blockbuster and Jacko's taproom of many beers, past the mysterious Chinese grocery that smells of déjà vu and is piled haphazardly and high with jars of Chinese herbs and small wooden boxes filled with strange dried and twisted roots, sits Marco's. It's down by the Shanghai Gardens Restaurant of greasy chow mein and possible stomach upset, past the two hairstylists that sit two doors apart, three or four blocks too far from the action in a more unfortunate stretch of the Avenue.

But do not doubt the fare, despite our lack of business. It's not for lack of heart or quality of risotto. We've got $20 ham in the walk-in and the freshest fish. Marco's is a restaurant of fine Chianti classicos and carpaccio, and Fridays still a packed house when we serve up his wife Gina's special fresh trenette with pesto. It's Marco's grandmother's recipe, the pesto, and I cannot divulge to you its exact ingredients because it was never made in the restaurant. It was the one big secret besides Gina's ladyfingers for her fabulous tiramisù. Both arrived whenever needed from home and, if you asked Gina, who all of us feared and some of us loved, she would give you that dark, nearly mad look of hers and wave you off with a gesture of her hand saying, "Oh, you know, the usual. Basil, garlic, pine nuts . . ." and then trail off and head to the prep room with her boiled and oven-dried potatoes for the gnocchi.

I started on a soup, minestra tricolore. I was chopping some fresh cauliflower and had onions cooking slowly in butter. The daily pot of polenta was bubbling slowly like molten yellow cornmeal lava, the radio was on and I had my first morning coffee. It's very peaceful the first hour and I'm nearly content.

Niko will be in around ten. She's morning prep/salad. Niko's a cute little African-American Oaktown woman. Maybe twenty-eight, thirty. She's small and wiry and always wears a tight T-shirt, no bra, you can see those firm little nipples pushing through until she covers up with the white dishwasher's shirt she wears. I wear one too. Gina didn't like it at first, but they're cooler than the heavy chefs' coats with their long sleeves and, besides, with the four-way apron cinched round your waist you can still cut a sharp figure and so Niko and me and the Mexican boys that wash the dishes wear the shirts and it has become a uniform we wear with pride. From the street instead of the Culinary Academy.

"Hey, baby." It's Niko come in out of nowhere already in uniform, she looks good in an apron wearing a big smile loaded with hot moist possibilities and then it's gone. White girls can't flirt like that. I don't know what it is.

"Coffee?" I asked.

"You know I don't like no coffee. Can't be drinkin' coffee. Bleah." She made a face.

"How can you deny coffee?" I asked. This is our morning ritual/flirt. I offer her coffee, she turns it down and then makes hot chocolate. Niko's been here for only a month and sometimes I dream on her "♪Ebony and Ivory . . . ♪"

"I don' know." She shook her head and began to heat up a pot of milk. Maxie the dishwasher liked hot cocoa in the morning, too, and my second espresso would be poured into a cup of that cocoa.

All was right with the world, we had the talk show on and there was a moment where Maxie was peeling and Niko was chopping and I was stirring some bubbling thing and no one said a word, working, waiting for the arrival of Marco who came in around eleven. He'd give us maybe five minutes more of our rock or R&B radio before the Italian opera and Italian-American crooner CDs came on. The time it'd take him to take off his coat and make himself his first and final cappuccino.

The doorbell rang and both Niko and I looked up from our work. Marco's was the kind of restaurant where they had a little bell that rang when the door opened. That was a sure sign that it wasn't the busiest of restaurants. A busy place doesn't need a bell. The door's opening and closing so often you only wonder when it's going to stop. You don't need a signal to look up from your paper and seat the stray couple that wandered into the place, probably by mistake. It was Marco carrying the morning bag of bread.

"Good morning, everybody." Marco came in looking a little tense and tired as he often did in the morning, being a person who came alive late at night.

Marco Lazerri was a small-framed man of about fifty with quick bright darting eyes and a thick head of grayish silver black hair and a mustache of the same color, both of which he tended to rather carefully in contrast to the more relaxed way he operated his restaurant.

He put down the bag of bread, checked himself in the small waiter mirror by the wine cooler, smoothed back his hair and mustache, looked himself in the eye again and then yelled toward the kitchen, "Well, who would like a coffee? A nice cappuccino?"

Marco's morning cappuccino was a very important beverage—to a man who took his beverages—particularly those that came from his greatly loved espresso machine—very seriously. No one could coax a shot of coffee out of that machine like Marco. Gina came close and if she asked me I'd say she was best just out of fear, but Marco was a true wizard with the milk-steaming knob. You could call his name and he'd never hear when he was lost in the foaming of the milk.

Marco was quite particular about the scheduling of the coffee drinks. It was cappuccino in the morning and machiattos or espressos from there on out except for an occasional latte just before bed. Marco was one of the few people who used coffee to go to sleep, but his family was from Genova after all.

He told me soon after I started, "Carlo," he said, "don't make a fool of yourself." He was shaking his head discreetly as though he didn't want the two old ladies sitting at table three to notice. I was making a cappuccino and it was two in the afternoon! At first I thought he was mad at me for going beyond my share, but actually it was a matter of decorum.

"Only in the morning. Cappuccinos are only for the morning. What is it with Americans? Machiatto. El Machiatto molti bueno." Whenever he spoke in Italian it was as though he were singing.

Marco made me an espresso, slid the tiny cup in front of me and then, like he was in a play, said "Machiatto?" and poised the steamed milk container above my cup.

"Si!" I said.

He poured in about two tablespoons of rich milk; Marco got the stuff with extra fat. Machiatto. Once we opened for lunch it was machiattos, espressos or nothing at all.

Marco went over the night's receipts while sipping on his coffee.

I watched him out of the corner of my eye as he took in the bad news. They'd done maybe thirty-two covers. Thirty-two people came in to eat our marvelous food. It was a damn shame.

The near-failing state of the place was one of the reasons I had taken the job in the first place. I'd reached the stage in my illustrious cooking "career" where I no longer sought the limelight, no longer dreamt of opening my own restaurant, writing my own cookbook, kicking Iron Chef's ass. While my Life Force/Ambition had not necessarily disappeared it was, like my libido, all dressed up with nowhere to go.

I think the problem was that I never aspired to be a chef from an early age or, for that matter, a late age. I didn't secretly play with my sister's Easy Bake oven, didn't wear pots on my head and bang on pans as a diapered toddler as did my younger brother, who incidentally turned that early fascination into a job with the GAO. But one's motives are carefully examined as you apply for the ten-dollar-an-hour job.

I remember I was asked no less than three times in my two interviews by Marco and Gina not only what great skills and talents I would bring to their restaurant, but why I became a chef. Why?

Of course I told them of a deep love of cooking and a near-religious reverence for food (this was somewhat true—I do love to cook and eat, it's just that the aneuryism-exploding, boiling-blood-pressure atmosphere of a busy kitchen at the height of a Friday night's rush for $80 take-home didn't really do much for me), but I couldn't reveal to them the reality. That if it wasn't for once living two blocks from a restaurant that made the tastiest slices of pizza in town I might have actually harnessed my brainpower for my own economic good. My Philosophical Mystery Question remains: Destiny or Dumb Luck?

It was a hippie-run pizza parlor in the old hood way down south before I found my fortune in the northern part of the state. They had great big slices of cheese pizza for a buck with the breadiest crust (which is my favorite; forgive me, crusty crust fans) and I used to eat there a lot with my First Major Girlfriend who later somehow roped me into moving to Monterey immediately prior to dumping me for a field hockey fan. One day the pizza place had a sign out for a delivery driver and I applied, needing a job and hoping for free slices.

"You got your own car?" I was asked by a thin, six-foot-plus guy with beard, photo-gray glasses and hair tied back that went down to the middle of his back.

"Yeah, Maverick. It runs great."

"Four seventy-five an hour, tips and you can take a pizza home every night."

"Cool." That's what I was after, free pizza.

He then took me aside and leaned toward me and asked, "Now, you smoke da kine?"

"Hmmm?"

"Kind bud."

"Green bud?"

He nodded. "You smoke it?"

"Sure!"

I was hired. He took me upstairs to show me where the pizza boxes were stored and the deal was sealed with a bubbler on the company bong that was the centerpiece of one of their two pieces of office furniture: a desk and a chair.

"Oh, one more thing." Long Hair looked up from the bong, wisps of smoke slipping out the sides of his mouth. "You can eat pizza 'til you can't shit anymore, but stay away from the ravioli."

I nodded, knowing nothing about either the ravioli or the constipatory powers of too much pizza, and embraced the first of the three great perks of restaurant work: food.

It turned out that the ravioli was handmade by Mel, one of the cooks, from an old New York family recipe. He made his own dough, ricotta and spinach filling, rolled it out by hand, cut them and dusted them with flour. All with the tender loving care of a young mother with a firstborn.

I was allowed one taste of the ravioli to shortcut terminal curiosity and was then told that that was it—remove any idea of the ravioli from your mind (they were amazing and I lusted after them more than I did for any of the waitresses). The raviolis were popular as hell and since they took forever to make and only Mel could make them just so, Mel was very protective of them and the first thing he did upon returning from his weekend was to count the number of ravs and compare it with the sales. If things didn't jibe he went from employee to employee to get to the bottom of it.

But I left the raviolis one day, ended up in the Bay Area (now migrating with Major Girlfriend Number Two who had been accepted at Cal) and parlayed my Italian cooking experience (which, in reality, mostly consisted of *delivering* the food rather than cooking it) into a position as lunch second-line cook at The Woodsman, one of those steak and baked potato houses that are done up like some fantasy hunting lodge.

I was suddenly in the trenches! Gone are the sunny San Diego days of pressing out an occasional pie, the slightly hectic delivery pace on a Saturday night (but come on! I was driving around listening to the tape deck blasting Clash). A dinner rush might have us backed up from time to time, but the bosses were hippies for chrissakes. They just didn't pack the DNA for a good fit. Long Hair's idea of a temper tantrum was, "Ya know, it might be a little cooler if you could go a little faster, ya know?" For this he always felt the need to apologize at the end of the night, giving me a bottle of beer and a pipeful before I went home. I could even guilt him into raviolis now and again ("Just don't tell Mel," he'd plead).

But West Oakland was an altogether different world. At The

Woodsman tags are coming in from an entire fleet of waitresses and there's only two of us trying to cook food at a frantic pace that made me feel like I was sinking into quicksand. I was waiting for hungry diners to break through the swinging doors separating the back from the front. They were like those freaky bugs in the disappointing *Starship Troopers*. Relentless. I had been introduced to the cooking concept of "going under."

Managers, a loathsome Life Form I'd never before encountered (typically balding white men in suits with fat faces and huge guts), would throw jowl-reverberating fits in the kitchen, usually at the busiest moments, like that was helping. Every time one of those assholes started reprimanding me all I could think was, "Fire me about six Monte Cristos." I could never keep up on the damn Monte Cristos. It was this egg-battered and deep-fried ham, chicken and cheese Wonder bread sandwich that might seduce the unwary to a shortened and sedentary life. At one point I had to make Jay, the day prep, swear he'd bitch-slap me if he ever saw me eating another. It got that close.

The managers were complemented by what was the first in a long and storied line of characters I came to know very well over time, becoming one myself at some point: Chef. This one, like many, was a miserable overworked barely human (salt mines always come to mind) dressed in checkers and whites. Chef Arnold, I can still see you *still* on your feet, leaning with all your lost life against the prep table. Even your mustache droops at 3 P.M. When he wasn't screaming or insulting one of us or questioning our intelligence, ability and parentage, Chef Arnold often had that worn look with the vacant/distant eyes of someone whom Life has beaten.

Luckily there was the prep crew. Mostly these homeboys from some of the toughest hoods around 98th and Edes. They supported and comforted me my first week with encouraging words such as:

"Check out the new white boy, cuz. How long you think this one last, E?"

Or the affirming:

"Wassamatta, cracker?! You cain't hang?"

Or, if they caught my eye, simply stared me down and made me look away thinking, No thank you. I don't want you to kill me.

But in the end, E and his cuz, Jay, were the only sane and fun and real thing in the whole job place. It was Jay who became my buddy and guide, introducing me to the art of grazing wherein the savvy and greedy kitchen employee might eat a fucking lot of expensive shit without getting fired. And it was Jay who taught me how to properly make the champagne sauce.

"All right here." Jay rubbed his hands together and tore open the case of champagne he'd had me carry out. Since I was new I didn't ask why we were going to the back parking lot to make a sauce.

Jay grabbed a bottle, tore off the wire and popped the plastic cork up and over the chain-link fence separating the parking lot and I-80, cars and semis whizzing by. He then looked around, poured a quick gulp into his mouth and poured the rest into the big stockpot. "Okay, you got it?"

"I think so."

"This is a very important sauce." Jay grinned and popped another plastic cork over the fence, took a drink and poured it into the pot. "Don' be fuckin' this sauce up. Aw right?"

It took a case of cheap ass sparkling wine—let's be fair to the French even if they don't deserve it—to make the sauce. At The Woodsman sauces were made in military-sized batches. Salad dressings required oars for stirring. We had a mixer the size of a grizzly bear that was strapped to the wall for the scary times when it was actually turned on and seemed to rumble and strain at the restraints, trying to bust free of The Woodsman's bonds. A story circulated involving a prep cook arm loss back in the early eighties. That's when they strapped her down.

Soon the "champagne sauce" became my favorite to prepare, stepping out after the lunch rush and popping those corks over the fence toward I-80 laughing, not caring if we got caught. They stopped us after a while. Management felt the same way about fun as did the Pennsylvania Dutch and cork popping in the back parking lot to make champagne sauce became officially prohibited, but we didn't care. Jay and I found new and better ways to goof off.

Jay clued me in to the fact that if you showed up vaguely on time and didn't strike anyone they'd keep you on indefinitely (throwing stuff was apparently okay as long as it wasn't real hard. For instance, a sauté pan at the manager's fat ass? You're at the unemployment office next morning. Try and wing the sous chef with a five-pound bag of au jus mix? Maybe a talking-to in the office and the postponement of your fifteen-cent-an-hour raise for yet another four months: For some reason The Woodsman's quarterly employee reviews took place three times a year).

What it boiled down to was that shenanigans did not result in termination at The Woodsman, but stealing was another matter. Stealing they worried about. And they worried about that quite a bit.

But Jay figured he had the perfect plan and soon rumors wafted through the kitchen that steak was disappearing in herd-sized quantities and management didn't own a clue because Jay had the foolproof system. He had it all worked out and I really couldn't argue with him.

"The Man" was keeping Jay down and there was no denying. He'd ask, "Now why you think I'm still a prep after all this time?" then he'd bust out his big laugh and that's how we became friends, laughing our asses off making fun of everybody else, dreaming about fucking the new waitress.

"Racism?" Being white it made me ill to say it. I had no other answer for why they never promoted him. Why "The Man" looked at him suspiciously all the time. Certain things happened to me that I never questioned because they always had and it was because of the color of my skin that they happened. A color I never considered because of the things I never had to question.

Jay decided that his most immediate and direct affirmative action in this case was to devise a system wherein he could make up any and all salary discrepancies and undercutting being performed by "The Man" upon Jay.

The Woodsman was paying him fifty cents over minimum after three years on the job (that's counting the six months where he was fired for threatening to kick Chef Arnold's ass), he explained to me over some fine iced tea at his auntie's, and I was completely behind him.

"They been ripping *me* off. I'm just evening it up," he told me. I'd sometimes give him a ride home, drop him off at a friend's or sometimes at his auntie's in the scary-to-the-white-boy neighborhood. We'd step out the car and the people would check out the white boy and inside we'd go into this neat and orderly fifties kind of fresh quiet home of doilies and family photos. A smell both clean and old-person musty and an immediate reverence and respect on Jay's part filled the house. We were as humble as the devout in church sitting at the Formica-and-chrome kitchen table.

Jay's target was the massive beef bounty delivered by the semi-load every Friday. This huge truck laden with cases and cases of Cryovac-ed USDA choice beef from our nation's heartland landed in West Oakland under direct order of Command Beef Central in the mile-high city of Denver. Top sirloins, New Yorks, Delmonicos, filets. They were all packed into cardboard boxes, each containing five sealed plastic bags filled with trimmed and weighed steaks.

Inventory of the beef delivery at The Woodsman was monitored as tightly as at a radioactive waste disposal site. All available managers stood watch over delivery like the overlords of some slave rowing crew and Chef Arnold counted up the shit, paying particular attention to the beef boxes as they came out of the truck. The Darkies (I'm fucking sorry—that's what it looked like to me. I was freakin' out!) unloaded the truck while White Trashy Ken and White Trashy Me cooked lunch at the usual extra frantic blood-sweat Friday pace.

After all was carefully unloaded and stocked and stored under futuristic controls (I kept looking for the secret hidden spy cameras) Caucasian males with clipboards (this became a job of mine one day) counted it all up again every few hours or so, walking through the storage areas and the walk-in refrigerators, pencil in hand.

The giant prime ribs, steaming and glistening, were carried from the alto-sham oven to the line like a delivery of gold bullion. The steel mesh-gloved prime rib carver (Miguel was the carver they all spoke of in revered tones; he worked weekend nights) had to file daily reports accurate to the ounce. Discrepancies on prime rib cut were discussed behind closed doors. Family men lost their jobs if they couldn't keep the cut tight. (Meanwhile, the prime rib steel mesh cutting glove kept disappearing at an alarming rate—this was during the height of Michael Jackson's career.)

The alcohol was even more precious than the meat, if that was possible. Cases of the hard stuff were delivered and stored practically under armed guard. Employees were never allowed drinks, especially the cooks, who when I arrived already had a deeply ingrained reputation for inability to control their rampant alcoholism. You could only drink in the bar after you clocked out, when it became the "Company Store for Alcohol." Except for unloading, the only time any of us in the back got close to the stuff was for "cooking" purposes. Hence our love of the champagne sauce and its once outdoor preparation.

But Jay didn't give a fuck about the alcohol; inventory was too tightly monitored. But the beef? Despite The Woodsman's safeguards and precautions, Jay came up with a plan that netted him cases of USDA prime corn-fed beef for months. He took advantage of his lowly position and his messiest job of the day.

Mopdown

Jay practically played up the "Yes'm massa" bullshit, with a big ol' "Yes'm massa I be in line now," fox-sly smile. It reminded me of *Cool Hand Luke*. And the GM even looked a little like a fat Strother Martin ("What we have is a failure to communicate.").

Jay'd mop around the whole back: kitchen, reefers, dry storage, Dumpsters, back room, all the way up to the hot tall blonde cashier who became my first taste of the second of the three great perks of restaurant life. There's no retirement, they don't give you medical or dental, paid vacation is a rare thing, you can't hardly even call in sick without engaging in a phone debate with the chef, but besides food there was another item on the menu: waitresses. Which, like Vegas slot machines, occasionally spill out: sex.

My job began to speak to me on a primal level (it remains hard to resist) and as per usual, Jay's mop took me to the cashier stand of the long tall full-breasted Darcy. I caught her eye again through the little passway where we put up all the plates.

And that was part of Jay's plan. You'd simply forget and not notice that it was Jay mopped you up to the big tall lean blonde; she was a D-cupped Texas-type freak from L.A. and I knew the right bands and my look filled her bill.

Meanwhile, all the time it's taking me to gain Darcy's pants Jay has mopped his way back to the walk-in, mopping the refrigerator floor, door closed, don't want to lose all that heat, it's cold as a muthafuck in here, like Fargo. No one's minding Jay. I'm looking

Darcy in the eye, the manager is sitting in the bar drinking (he's fucking the bookkeeper, that fat old muthafuck, she was alright), chef is patrolling the kitchen wondering which of the dark-skinned were ripping him off, driving up his food costs, taking money outta his bonus! His mustache drooping all the more.

It didn't last, me and the cashier. She dumped me cold one day hard outta the saddle after some hot fucks and I had that pussy-free funk hanging over me heavily, but Jay meanwhile had stock-piled huge inventories of beef! While some dealt in crack and dime bags of endo, Jay was making a name for himself on the streets of West Oakland as the man to go to for a fine steak. He was netting way more weekly than the chef even.

It was finally revealed to me. I never guessed. I was doing inventory and wondering why some of the bottom cases weren't full, wondering why the last idiot couldn't do a good inventory and meanwhile Jay's stashing stacks of sealed steak bags in the bottom of his filthy mop bucket during mopdown, wheeling it outside, stashing the meat in some tall grass behind the Dumpster and then retrieving it later that night.

Jay pulled one out one day; this was after I'd quit and ended up in a fine restaurant, a famous restaurant in Berkeley. I was visiting and gave him a ride home and as we sat in my car in front of his auntie's house, he pulled a Cryovac of New Yorks out of his pack.

"You should see the look on your face." He laughed and did some pantomime of bug eyes and slack jaw. "Your jaw just dropped."

He told me the whole story and we were both laughing and I thanked him and took the Cryos of New York steaks home and cooked them up for some friends. I don't know what Jay does these days.

mike and kat

So I went to the bar to visit my pal, Mikey.   We were to meet at
Jacko's and I walked into the place hoping Mike and Kat had
broken up. That they were on the outs and Mike could crash at my
pad for a while and we'd drink lots of beer and have bitches in the
livin' room 'til 3 in the mornin'.

Mike was supposed to have been my big bachelor buddy. I had
it all pictured. It was all figured out, but he gets hooked up soon
as I get ca-, as soon as . . . She and I were no longer together, right
after Mike tells me about the benefits of not giving a shit, he hooks
up with this dumb ass chick with a big rack who was offering free
rent.

"I'm moving in with Kat." He said it in this matter-of-fact,
tough-guy manner in the third week of January. Like there was
nothing to it.

My jaw near dropped. Mike had always philosophized at great
lengths on the benefits of singledom, chasing the pussy, woman as
mere problem-laden pussy possessors that wielded no power over
our gender save for the possession of said pussy and here I was at
long last free of monogamy's bonds and he goes and hitches. Bitch!

"I need a place right now and there's a garage for my motorcycle." He said it mealy-mouthed, like that was his main motivation.

The garage. The bennie that made the difference. That got him to move in with Kat.

"You're moving in with Kat?" I couldn't fucking believe it.

"Yeah."

"No way."

"I'm serious."

I just looked at him.

"What?!" he said angrily. "What's the big fuckin' deal anyway?! I just wanna save on some rent. I want to go overseas and teach English is what I really want to do."

"What about not giving a shit?"

Mike just shrugged.

In an instant all my plans were ruined. Mike ruined all my plans by moving in with Kat. Mike and me *both* being single was one of the bright spots of my plan. Well, it wasn't exactly a plan in the sense that I was an active agent or initiator—planner if you will—of any kind, but there *was* an after-the-fact plan and that plan was, "Fuck Love." The plan was to fuck love and just fuckin' pick up on girls. Have the ladies swoonin' and pinin' and givin' it up. It was all Mike talked about while . . . She was living with me. I could almost lay a portion of my Trial with Monogamy at Mike's feet.

All his single man freedom talk while glaring at a woman's tight ass as she walked by or the meeting of eyes intense, pheromonic and false? It goaded me on, I tell you.

But at least we could still talk about chicks and shit because, frankly, as soon as he hooks up with Kat, Mike's talking about chicks all the time. Even more so if that's possible because now they're just a bit more ripe and available, practically oozing all over the place. If only he were a free man. There was many a time that he'd say to me, "If I was only single."

But I was and that's why it just wasn't the Bachelor Duo I'd pictured. He'd either bitch about his woman or goad me on to the imagined fantastical boldness levels he claimed to have once practiced when he was single. Levels I knew to be total fabrications. We'd argue about it sometimes and then he'd say, "Yeah, but you're not even fucking anybody."

I'd get silent and go sour for a while.

See? That's no Swingin' Bachelor Duo.

I stepped inside the joint looking for Mike. I was a bit excited because I had things to tell him. There was still an anxious air about this Russian woman and I wanted to tell him about her. Play up that Russian angle. It has *me* excited. The former ill will our countries once held for one another gives this wanna-be affair a certain verboten edge that I like and I can't wait to tell Mike about both her brain and her ass.

But who catches my eye? Kat. I see her sitting next to him in that clingy way she has about her. She's a pointy little blonde with jutting elbows and collarbones and a delicate neck and arms and then, shapang! she's fucking stacked. I knew that and the free rent were Mike's main consideration. I knew it but didn't say it because guys didn't even like to admit that shit to each other (at least not the free-rent part).

"Dude, what's up? Where you been?" Mike's all excited to be out even if his woman is there. We're just drinkin' and shooting a game of pool or some darts is all. Kat'll sit off to the side in that clingy way of hers, hardly saying a word.

"Hey." I nod toward them. Can they tell I slip a little when I see that she's there? Probably not. Mikey just wants to have a beer and shoot a game of pool and Kat's main concern is keeping an eye on Mike.

"So Mike tells me you're seeing this Russian woman?" Kat asks after I rejoin them with my pint. All forms of romance intrigue

Kat endlessly. That and the whereabouts of Mike when he's out of her sight are all that really interest her.

"Yeah," I say somewhat excitedly. I'll tell Kat about Anastasia's brain and then when Kat goes to the bathroom, try and fit in the part about Anastasia's ass with Mike.

"Is she nice?"

"Yeah, she's pretty nice. Really smart," I answer.

"So when do we get to meet her?"

"Mmmm, I don't know," I answer, thinking, Probably not before I sleep with her.

Luckily after a bit of this Kat excuses herself to go to the bathroom and Mike and I practically burst forth with what we really have to say.

"So, how's things with the wife?" I ask sarcastically.

"She's not my wife, all right?!" He looked around the bar in an almost angry eagerness. "She's drivin' me fuckin' nuts, man." Mikey seemed rather fed up, but then he did walk into the relationship half fed up. "It's like my mother. 'Where are you going?' 'When are you coming back?' Shit!"

"She was fuckin' drivin' you nuts before you ever moved in with her," I comforted him with that special man-to-man tenderness.

"Yeah . . . I fuckin' know that, all right?" he exploded, and then said more quietly, looking down into his glass of beer, "At least I'm gettin' some." Then he drained his pint and wiped his mouth with the back of his shirted forearm.

I went sour for a second. "Man, this Russian chick. Did I tell you—," I tried to rally.

"Look at that chick. Look at her waist," Mike said as a hottie walked by. "Damn! She was eyein' me, dude."

"Nice. This Russian chick . . ."

"Wup, here comes Kat. Lay off the chick talk."

Kat sat down next to Mike, clutched his arm in that clingy way she had with him and scanned the bar for potential hot chicks.

They weren't like . . . She and I. As far as a couple went. I could see Mike was just biding his time. But I didn't really feel like thinking about that kind of stuff, what kind of a couple they were. What kind of a couple . . . She and I had once been. Luckily a pool table opened up for us.

friday night

On Friday night Marco's was transformed from its sleepy weekday self into a real restaurant. Once a week the place could be counted on to be packed and busy, with high tension and good food. And at closing Marco was always happy enough with the business for a bottle of wine with the crew and we might talk late into the night about everything serious and funny we could imagine, but before that sweet moment late in the evening, rendered all the more sweet by the extra sweat we'd poured for the cause, Fridays were the worst, man. We'd bust our ass as the restaurant packed up and buzzed with weekend excitement. Half our business took place on Friday and Saturday night.

Gina took Friday very seriously, but this day had been sunny which always brightened her, so I was hoping. My first thought as I stepped into the dry storage area to change was, What sort of mood is Gina in? Niko was rummaging through the reefer.

"Hey, Niko. What's up?"

She slammed some romaine into a bus tub, looked up at me, rolled her eyes, a shitty look on her face, and stormed off. Uh-oh.

Typical Friday. I always fully expected to walk in and hear some yelling or grumbling amongst the troops on Friday. Friday was the day all the cooks entertained notions of walking. Just quitting and finding some better life where one might dine out on a weekend evening rather than toiling and sweating in the heat and smoke of the kitchen.

Gina was in the small prep room making the fresh trenette for Friday's pesto special. It's a long noodle. She had her well of flour built on the large wood table with the egg and water and salt in the middle.

"Now watch," she told me without so much as a hello, only looking up at the clock to see if I was on time. "You want to mix it slowly at first. Scrapping the edges of the flour into the liquid. You can't break the wall, huh?"

"Unh-unh," I answered.

She continued working the flour into the middle with her fork and it began to thicken into a dull yellow ball, shiny with the yolk. After a time she had worked in enough flour to be able to pick it up.

"Now you have to scrap the table, eh? Are you listening?"

"Yeah," I said.

"This is very important." She looked at me seriously and then commenced to scrap the table clean, deposit it all in a strainer and sift the flour back onto the board and toss out the globs. She then worked in a little more flour and began to knead it. "Not too much flour. When you start you always think you need more flour, but you don't. Here. For five minutes."

I was to knead it by hand. Gina avoided kitchen appliances whenever possible ("You have to get a feel for the food if you want to know it," her hands held like claws to the sky). She wanted me to do it by hand, roll it out with the heels of my hands, fold it over, turn it and do it again and again until the dough began to become elastic and lively.

"It's three 'til. I'll be back at two after and we'll see what we have," and Gina left the room. "And then I want that shark broken down. Let's move! It's going to be busy tonight. Where'd Niko go? Niko!"

Five minutes of kneading pasta is like going to Gold's gym out of the blue after seven straight years of absolutely no activity. Your upper arms go first and that's when you slow down and learn right then to start slower next time.

"That woman needs to chill the fuck out." Niko came into the kitchen shaking her head, carrying a case of artichokes to prep. She leaned toward me and said quietly, just in case, "It wouldn't kill her to smile once or twice."

Gina did have a temper. It could peel wallpaper. All of a sudden she would turn on you like a rabid dog in the middle of service when the orders were pouring in and the pans were loaded with food and sizzling and the grill was packed and smokin'. It was like she hated you suddenly because everything wasn't quite perfect. It was never quite perfect.

We were all subject to the moods of Gina. If Gina was having a bad enough time, well then by God so was everybody else, and if our funny good time just didn't strike her right at just the right time, well then watch out. She'd machine-gun some shit at you with her accent and dark brow and, well, you could fry an egg on top of her forehead sometimes and often on Friday when we prepared the meals that were a little more special because the weekend was special, especially at Marco's where the business during the week just wasn't.

"She's Sicilian; that's how they are" was my explanation for Niko.

"Well, if they all like that"—Niko was all sassy—"then you best be takin' Sicily off the damn itinerary. No need to be goin' there. Unh-unh."

Gina was Sicilian and actually from Italy whereas Marco in reality grew up in the States though he was born in Genova and while Marco came alive with his Italian heritage (even the accent he'd fall into sometimes, though we all knew he was from some big Midwestern city), with Gina it just was. There was nothing to prove beyond the expatriate's usual burden.

She came from the south country, while Marco's family came from the north, the seaport of Genova, home of Cristoforo Colombo and his mamma's old family secret recipe focaccia and pesto. But this is about Gina, see how Marco would always butt in when it came to be about Gina? That's his nature, but Gina can stand free and strong on her own. She's as tall as Marco who was wiry and almost short, his gray mustache and prematurely gray hair in contrast to Gina's dark olive vitality ten years his junior.

And Gina, in the end, and pretty much in the beginning, too, was the boss and supreme ruler of, if not the restaurant, then the kitchen, which is where I lived in this book. So, in my eyes, Gina ruled.

"Okay, let's see what you have," Gina said as she came back into the kitchen. Niko looked down trying to get a pout across, but Gina had no time or use for it. We were opening in two hours. "Have you been kneading the whole time?"

"Yep."

She picked up the big ball of dough, which was now very shiny and plastic-looking. "You didn't use too much flour did you?"

"Hardly any."

"Clean the board. Here's the shark. We need a sauce for it. Make it something good."

I could hardly believe it. We had mako shark *and* Gina rewarded me with a sauce decision. A fat quarter loin, twelve pounds or so, lay moist, almost shimmering on my cutting board. I love mako. I believe it to be one of the tastiest fishes in all the Pacific. Lone swimmer out in the middle of that vast ocean, caught by accident in the commercial fisherman's miles-long raping nets.

It was my job to break down the fish even though our grill man,

Rock'n'Rollero, would probably use it because Gina knew I could butcher a fish and Rock'n'Rollero sucks. With my twelve-inch slicing knife it was soon skin and a couple of corner bits and six-to-seven ounce portions and, of course, that one piece. The extra pretty one. For Marco.

Marco was a seafood man and had a second sense when the fish was being broken down and soon appeared in the prep room. I'd catch him watching over my shoulder as I portioned. At first I thought he was some asshole boss making sure nothing is lost or stolen, but he was only excited by the process, his mouth watering for the fresh grilled fish that would be his 3 P.M. lunch. He'd often clap me on the back at the end with, "Bellisimo. Gina, I told you this boy can use a knife!" and he'd take that prime slice and salt and pepper it, rub it with olive oil and throw it on our small woodburning grill.

And Gina would have me taste it, have me taste any dish she was particularly excited about. "Taste this," she'd say, tough and confident. "See what you're serving tonight. If you don't like it neither will the customer."

Mako's the best. Gina said it tasted more like the swordfish in the Mediterranean than did the Pacific stuff. I decided to make a rustic sauce of roasted tomato, black olives, capers and garlic slivers with chopped Italian parsley at the very end. With the top secret-pesto on our fresh trenette and a classic Milanese risotto Gina whipped up, we had the usual great Friday menu planned out.

By seven o'clock the place was packed and for once Marco's rang with not merely the sad occasional ding of the door's bell, but with the sounds of a real restaurant. The door to the kitchen would swing open, a waiter would appear to fire an order and the sounds would slip in. Claire would disappear with two plates full of food and you'd hear it. Along with the announcement "Order in!" you'd hear the sounds of a restaurant come alive, the hum of the diners, the clacking of forks and knives against plates, the tinkling of glasses, the crash of dirty plates being dumped into bus tubs, the gentle and sometimes loud bits of conversations over the general buzzing backdrop that arose whenever capacity was reached. Laughs, coughs, the occasional dreaded crash of something being dropped, a note of Marco's voice, the singular mingling of a large group of people in the fun mode of out on the town and a smaller group sweating under the weight of it all.

Time slipped and in twenty minutes it had gone from six to ten. It's the end of the night. I'm still in my checkered pants, but a fresh shirt and sitting at "the Table" with Marco, Dave—his philosophizing wild-mushroom-and-abalone-procuring buddy—and Moira, our latest third waitress.

The waitress crew numbered only three because the business wasn't what they wanted, wasn't what it should have been for the fine food served. (Because of the slow business Marco waited on tables most weeknights—"If it wasn't for the tips I don't know what Gina and me'd do sometimes," he'd confess to me when he'd had a few glasses.)

There was Claire who was gay and worked weekend nights and while the cockiest of the cooks, like Rock'n'Rollero, felt he might entice her to switch sides, such was not to be. And there was Ramona, the main lunch waitress who was just a little too strange for any of us to entertain any erotic notions about, and then there was the third waitress. It was the spot on the roster that never got filled. The scapegoat waitress, the transient plate carrier and order taker.

In the nine months I'd been there we'd gone through about six third waitresses. We even tried a waiter for a while, it got so desperate, but nobody liked that so we went back to the revolving third waitress routine. Marco kept trying to hire slutty flirtatious ones. Monica Lewinsky types, but Gina was looking more for someone along the lines of, say, a young Janet Reno.

Moira, the latest, was regaling the boys at "the Table" and Marco and I granted her audience as though she were Oscar Wilde stopping by for a chat. She was explaining that, yes, she was an aspiring actress and had met David Mamet or maybe it was a second cousin of David Mamet. I forget, but either way she'd been trained in the thespian arts and had the smoothest skin and most wonderful expression. Her mouth was filled with Welcome Wagon.

The new girl. The new girl was especially hot as a result of her newness—before the fact that she wasn't going to sleep with any of us (or only one of us, tops) came out and kind of soured most of the crew on her. But in the beginning, like tonight, it was an Oktoberfest of love and fucking fantasy starring the new girl and she'd be practically bombarded by all the attention, and the waitresses who'd been around a while, who were now complete actual human beings to most of the men, always seemed a bit jealous of the new girl. Unless she was fat or ugly. Then they liked her straight off.

el niño

It's Tuesday afternoon. My favorite moment in my entire world for the past few months. It's three o'clock and I have a full belly from work which I've just left, oh, say fifteen minutes ago. I don't return until Friday afternoon. Ahh.

But it's already October and winter is coming. There's no denying this despite the fact that I'm walking down the Avenue in a T-shirt sweltering in 85-degree mid-October sun. That day's sunset would be record-breaking breathtaking and I bask in its splendor until I step inside the publick house, Jacko's, and my mind locks and loads on beer and the coming winter.

I always had a beer upon leaving work on Tuesday. It's one of the three imperatives of my existence. I'll tell you about the other two later.

The man taps me my beer and I right off commence on the second of my three imperatives. Women. Winter is coming and I remain squeezeless. Standard time returns next Sunday and according to the latest from the meteorologists, the weather will not be in my favor this year.

It's fucking El Niño. This pounding heat in mid-October, the troublesome nature of girls this year? It's nearly the hottest day of the entire year and that can only mean the rains will be that much heavier. I have to act fast.

As I sip a fine Moylan's hand-pumped bitter I remember that down off Torrey Pines the waters were mid-seventies in August— I was down there!—and the sun was booming on the flat sand beaches, shining down hard, big waves even rolled in swollen from some hurricane brewing off the tip of Baja chugging north (The Child was fussin' back then; I cheered El Niño) and the warm water dripped off me as I walked back to shore after rising and falling with the warm swells. I walked back in kicking at the water that flowed past and drew back from my knees, to my calves and then down to my ankles as I made my way up the wet sand, through the moist sand (the little kids making sand castles were so cute; I eyed their mothers lasciviously nonetheless), to the hot dry sand, past those two hotties oiled and buns up on their towels (they're trying to catch an eye) and made my way to my own towel to lie down into the face up closed-eyes heat of this perfect Southern Californian moment.

But today, despite the misleading warmth, I have maybe three, four weeks before the weather changes and the women (who unlike myself can sexually hibernate for entire seasons without so much as knitting a brow) shut down for the year. They'll lie dormant, gaining strength for April. My sexuality is of a less deciduous nature and not nearly so patient. I should just listen to Niko: "This Anastasia has gots to go! She had best be steppin'. How long you been goin' out? And you ain't gettin' none?!"

I was not making the best choices. Anastasia mostly operates on the Mount Everest Principle. Tenzing Norgay, baby. She's there! Unfortunately, my attempt at finding out what sort of panties foreign-born intellectuals wear is proving a bit more involved than first hoped for (especially since my first hopes pretty much involved the delving into of moist folds by the third date), but I have an ace up my sleeve. A Hot Date with Anastasia wherein back at my house I woo her with a smashingly moist and light soufflé followed by a warm and creamy zabaglione. I drain the beer, wipe my mouth with the back of my sleeve and head home. She doesn't stand a chance. The U.S. is gonna kick Russia's ass again.

the soufflé

We're at the lake where Anastasia likes to go. Her, me and her gigantic dog. Anastasia has this aged pony-sized dog with bad skin. It's far too large for the size of her apartment which might have been four hundred square feet at best. Perhaps this seems palatial to a Russian Jewess from Moscow who's just left a fallen empire. Maybe she thinks that's plenty of room for a 125-pound dog that stands six-foot-seven on its hind legs. I don't know. I now avoid politics completely after once casually offering the astute politico-historical analysis that V.I. Lenin was "a pretty cool guy."

"Vell, yes"—she looked at me disgustedly—"if you like mass murderers." Ever since then we've limited political discussions to her harangues about how stupid everything is in the United States. Anastasia never uses the article "the" when referring to my home-land. It's always, "In United States no one reads," or, "In United States with your TV . . ."

It was hard to disagree with her shock at our lack of culture and education, but I decided if she ever pushed it too far I'd defend this great land of ours by saying, "Then why the fuck did you move here?! Fuckin' pack your bust-ass back on the next plane if you don't like it, bee-yach!" But I wisely decided to save my patriotism for the breakup.

Either way, at the lake she was giving far more attention to her dog than I was emotionally prepared for. Frankly, on this, our fifth date, I'd thought the attention might be focused quite a bit on me, but I let it slide, figuring to cash in on this lack of attention later on the couch after I've prepared her dinner. I've got the whole thing wired.

We're going back to my place. All chairs have been locked in the garage, leaving the one chair that wouldn't fit through the door easily enough (but I've piled it with tons of crap, rendering it useless) and a small couch. The champagne is chilling and I've decided to go with the risky but potentially impressive soufflé.

I'm beating the egg whites in a copper bowl in the golden dusk's light that filters into my west-facing kitchen window. Anastasia stands watching me wryly, wineglass in hand, a soft beauty nearly obscured by her naturally dour nature.

It came out beautifully. The soufflé. I love to beat egg whites into fluffy peaks. They say your whisk should never strike the bottom of the bowl, a silent beating being the best of all. I had some Reggiano I'd "borrowed" from work and my béchamel to bind it. The dish came out of the oven swollen far above the rim of my soufflé pan. A gorgeous golden brown.

We're sitting mere millimeters apart on the couch. The soufflé was moist, the champagne dry. I gambled with *Swept Away* (foreign films are all she'll have; she seems to hate everything about American culture and things American except living here and it was one of my top three Italian films, not being real big on Fellini). I thought the stunning color photography combined with the consummated sexual tension might pay off, but I think it backfired. The movie only seemed to rile up Anastasia.

My hopes for that evening (even though it feels like it's been so long that my brain has literally morphed into a penis. It's all dick up there; I can barely discuss the pros and cons of the dialogue and

Guarnieri's gorgeous film photography) were no greater a goal than the mild "feeling up" of this former Communist. A few kisses leading to some tongue work, culminating with some lingering breast fondlage (over the clothes of course), was all that I asked. I'd pared expectations down to that level 289 days later.

Well, Anastasia loved the soufflé, claimed the champagne was a demi-sec (no, it's brut. Don't question me about food!) and then got fussy when Mariangela Melato begged to be sodomized, labeling all Italians decadent. I guess the fantasy of being stuck on an island with Giancarlo Giannini and the specter of anal sex didn't preheat her ovens because there was nothing much in her kisses. As always I ignore this and press onward until she tells me that she wants to go slow. (Slow?! I think, It's *already* slow. Those two on the desert island are getting more action. I don't know what you call slow in Russia, but here in the good old U S of A this is plenty goddamn slow!)

"Okay," I say meekly and reach for my champagne flute.

While she persistently—and, at first, calmly—pushed my hands away from anything beyond her arm, she continued with the conversation. Well, it was more like a lecture, really.

Anastasia was some sort of Russian/*Star Trek* brainiac. I kept trying to locate the huge throbbing veins pulsating along the sides of her head. There couldn't possibly be any blood allocated for her clitoris, I was thinking while she schooled me about poetry, psychology and history. I wondered what sort of school systems the Soviets must have run. If they had the money they would have kicked our asses and it made me dream on the inner workings of her heart, what it was like inside there. I pictured it a frozen white expanse. I saw a little girl intellectual in her now crystal-clear steel blue eyes and the utter expressionlessness of her face right then mesmerized me and I fell in love for a brief moment as I often will on a couch.

"There is the phlegmatic . . . ," she explained again.

"The melancholic," I interrupted excitedly, "the choleric and, what's the other?"

"The sanguinic."

"The most integrated of them all."

"Vell, yes. Of course." She finished rolling up one of her Russian joints. She'd empty one of the fat Russian cigarettes and mix some Northern Cali outdoor-grown green bud in with the tobacco and pack it back in. She was very methodical about it. She held the joint tightly between her lips and stuck it out toward the lighter with her mouth. She was a smoker and in a strange way her thin face, when she drew in the first drag, had the look of death about it, like the cigarette was sucking on her.

As she told me about self-actualizing and the ideal spontaneous person (someone I wanted to be that night. It sounded so brilliant, the true spontaneous person living in a content excitable state), I followed this spontaneity with my fingertips walking up her arm and stroked her tricep with the back of my hand.

Nothing.

I leaned toward her neck until I could feel the Slavic heat coming off it. She remained as still as a statue.

WROOF!! WROOF-WROOF!!

Her gigantic dog always seemed to perk up whenever I got too close. His ears would stand at attention and he'd laboriously pick up his eighty-four-in-dog-years ass off the carpet and give me the impression that it was taking all his years of Soviet obedience training (helped along by his severe arthritic condition) to *not* lunge at my throat to defend his mistress.

"Oh, Pavel wants some attention." Anastasia came alive, now filled with the full warmth of life, and got up to pet the dog. She returned to the couch and sat down ten centimeters farther away from me than when she got up.

Looking back, I now realize that the two of them were tag-teaming me out of any fleshy fun. I meant no harm, but nowhere we go, it's all brain tonight and would be the next time. She'd kiss me dead fish and that was that.

I don't know. She still wanted to chat on the phone, go out and do things, but . . .

She didn't get it. Sometimes they simply don't get it. Sometimes a man is first on the hunt and nothing can sway him from the quarry of the wet warmth between a woman's thighs. And with this El Niño thing, well, there's just not a lot of fucking time for "friends" sometimes. Is that so bad?

leftover soufflé

My solipsism was again getting the better of me. I didn't take it to the extreme and believe that only I was real, that everything around me was as though a dream, props merely for my own pleasure or displeasure. I knew that others existed outside of my sight. I knew there were worlds independent of me—it's just that I could be sure of none of it. All the rest was simple speculation and so, in a sense, I *was* my only reality.

So in this solipsistic state I headed out of the house, the second day of my weekend already winding down and the balking of Anastasia still a bitter pill. I headed to the Chaat house to meet another good buddy, Neil, who, while getting close to achieving true agoraphobia, had actually been coaxed into meeting two of his oldest pals out in public.

Neil was to be escorted by Mike from the bus stop near his work to the Chaat House. No one was *ever* allowed to meet Neil at either his place of residence or his work. He was very explicit about this. No one could visit him at work and no calls were ever to be made there. It just wasn't done. Management wasn't keen on that sort of thing, Neil tried to convince us.

As I entered the Chaat House, licking my lips at the smell and visions of soon eating a fantastic samosa cholle, I saw they already had a table and that Mike, who could not accept Neil's work visitation claims, was already going at him.

M: What is anyone gonna say? Your coworker sweeps for a living. How can he dog you?

Neil shook his head and did that nervous nose rub of his.

M: What if I met you in the parking lot next time?

N: Forget it, Mike!

M: Why can't I just come and see where you work?

N: There's no room there for visiting.

M: You work in a warehouse. Only flight hangars are bigger.

N: There's a lot of carpet there. Way too much. They keep ordering more and more carpet and . . . well, it's filling up the whole damn place.

M: Come on, how can—

N: Don't tell me about the carpet business, Mikey! What do you know about carpets?! And what can you possibly tell me about warehouses that I don't already know?

M: I'm not trying to tell you about the carpet business, goddamn it! How 'bout if I just drive by?

N: Forget it!

M: On your days off then. Just slow down a little. I won't even get out of the car. How can that be any sort of a problem?

I could see that if Mike kept pushing it he was gonna blow the whole thing and then wondered if maybe I wasn't being aggressive enough with my recent dates. Perhaps the night *should* end in a shove backwards if not an embrace. I pulled up a chair.

C: Would you guys fucking shut up and at least let me eat my samosas in peace if you're only gonna bicker.

N: Hey, what's up? Only if you promise not to talk about Karen.

Ouch, I think, as a vision of . . . her and a flash of uncomfortable silence fills the place.

M: Or sports. Please.

C: Mmmm . . .

I dug into a samosa they'd ordered and in about ten seconds we ended up somehow talking about women anyway.

M: It's like this—women are like a cake mix for life.

C: Say what?!

M: Yeah, a woman can sort of set things up, get the ball rollin'.

N: Why a cake mix, Mikey? What's cake got to do with anything?

M: Well, who wants to be going around makin' shit from scratch?

C: So, how's your baking been going, Mike?

M: Oh, shit. Don't even get me started on Kat, all right? I'm sure she'll be paging me here any minute.

Kat. Kat bugged me. I had it in for Kat. Yeah, don't even get me (or Mike for that matter) started on Kat.

M: Then on top of it I met this little hottie at the Jack in the Box drive-through. She even slips me free tacos sometimes.

N: I like their tacos. How come McDonald's doesn't do one?

M: They always show up when you got somebody. When you're alone they're . . .

C: Like cops.

N: Never around when you need 'em.

We all laugh.

M: This Jack in the Box chick though . . . Sometimes I just wanna rip her little wireless headset off and tear that shit up. You know those billboards with the tacos?

C: Yeah . . .

M: Just the sight of one of those and I got wood now.

N: I see you still go for non–college graduates.

M: At least I don't live in the Bat Cave with Secret Woman. I know more about those Roswell aliens than about your woman.

Not only had none of us ever seen where Neil worked, only one of us had ever been inside any residence he had ever lived in the entire time we knew him and some of us had known him for fifteen years.

As far as Neil's "woman," the only evidence any of us had ever seen was a tattered black and white he'd once whipped out for an instant. I'm still fairly certain it was a newspaper clipping or year-book photo.

N: So, who you seein', Carrasco?

C: Oh, man, lemme tell you about this Russian chick.

N: A Russian?

C: Yeah.

N: Cool.

As I played up (embellished, fabricated, whatever) the story I had another "attack." It's hard to describe, really. It's a physical tired-ness, but behind this lack of energy looms an enigmatic anxiety and complicating matters even more (besides the fact that whatever physical symptoms play over my body, in truth I believe it to be a sickness of the soul) is trying to maintain some semblance of composure when an attack takes place in public.

In the midst of my lies about Anastasia and how much she wanted me (couldn't get enough of my American dick; boy, I played it up in an attempt to stay connected) my life again took on pre-posterous dimensions. My life became . . . larger than life. I'm a gigantic Macy's Thanksgiving Parade Bullwinkle float, moving clumsily through time, space and a nasty downdraft. A mindless smile of goodwill is plastered on my face as the conversation thank-fully faded away from me.

M: There's bands in Britain that we don't even know about here.

N: That's 'cause nobody listens to 'em over there either.

M: No! There's bands that have entire careers, popular bands, that we never hear.

N: No way!

M: It's true.

N: Name one.

M: I don't know their names.

N: Un-huh.

M: I just told you, we don't know about them here so how the fuck could I possibly know their names?! Damn! How many people in Britain you think've heard of Urkel?

I was slipping in and out of an existential crisis vortex as they went on and on and on, trying to put my larger-than-life life back into the bottle. I almost visibly gasped for air as the two of them finally reached an angry consensus against the use of the words "rock and roll" and its definition in the songs of Billy Joel *or* Huey Lewis.

The atmosphere in the pub became close and thick and a wave of dreamy dizziness drifted before my teetering consciousness. I reached for a poori and took a bite. That was good. The poori was warm and moist. The food filled my working mouth. My weekend was about over.

Mike drove Neil to near his home and I headed back to my place with, of course, the impossible fantasy of finding the instant, new and improved girl of my dreams on the walk home and, of course, such was not the case.

Now that I'd given up any hope of Anastasia, no pussy was killing me again. Oh, I know it hadn't been *that* long, but it's not like a bank account. It had only been ninety-two days, but you can't stockpile the shit. Ten months with hardly *a* girl (or wrecky liaisons like Maria Cordova) after being with *The* Girl. Or so I thought. I'm not sure *The* Girl is *The* Girl if it doesn't last. Can *The* Girl just drop you? What could that possibly mean? To finally meet *The* Girl only to discover you're not *The* Guy.

My mind drifted back to . . . Her.

AIYEEEH!! AIYEEEH!!

The Monster . . . SHE

The monster . . . She (**AIYEEEH!! AIYEEEH!!**) didn't start out so monstrous. It didn't begin with her crawling out of the depths and fog of crushed love to rip my beating heart out and unleash her Godzilla/Banshee wail,

"**AIYEEEH!! AIYEEEH!!**"

But that is what . . . She has become. . . . SHE walks the streets of the City now and to picture her in her former form as K——— is but to fall prey to her touchless mind-meld poison.

Oh, no. I'm not so easily fooled. Tonight she is monstrous indeed, plunging her raptor claw right through my breastbone, pulling out in one fell swoop my still-beating heart, crushing it in her reptilian paw, tossing it to the ground and then inadvertently (for despite the depths of my own pain, it is nothing to . . . Her— **AIYEEEH!! AIYEEEH!!**) stepping on it as she plods away, looking for more mayhem, more fresh beating hearts still capable of the Love that she so craves, so craves to crush.

AIYEEEH!! AIYEEEH!!

She can expose the fraud of my "Fuck Love" persona, make me think sometimes in sad nostalgia of the summer mornings when we'd sit out in the backyard with our coffee and a special pastry that I thought meant "Us."

But I'm getting ahead of myself here. While the story may (or may not; I'm not willing to admit) begin with . . . Her— **AIYEEEH!! AIYEEEH!!**

while it may, in fact, fucking revolve around . . . Her, it really begins tonight and that morning in August and in the fresh satiated aftermath of Maria Cordova. It begins, always, on the days when I again find myself washed up on the shores of now, broken up and alone. Days that always hit me out of the blue, a ton o' bricks, despite their overdue nature.

I walked past the video store and made the mistake of falling for the neon sign, the brightly lit interior and racks of exciting video boxes with all their colors and promise.

I stepped inside and there was the heartbreakingly beautiful young blonde girl who'd just been hired and I tried my best to ignore her and after a halfhearted browse of the French films (wishing I was Daniel Auteuil, that Emmanuelle Beart had once loved *me*) I headed to the classics. There it was. I knew it wasn't the best time, but it practically popped off the shelf at me and I was weak-willed. With a vengeance I grabbed my Number Two Most Romantic Movie of All Time.

Alfred Hitchcock's *Notorious*.

I would head home and crank up the heat and turn off the phone (fuck her if she—any of the various shes—tries to call. Fuck 'em all). I'm gonna turn down the lights, turn off the phone and turn on the movie. I want to see Ingrid Bergman in Ted Tetzlaff's soft focus dying from unrequited love and the poison potion administered by Madame Sebastian, my favorite Leopoldine Konstantin role, for tomorrow is work and tonight let me at least have my dreams of wonderful love if I can't get even any half-assed sex.

I'll love you, Ms. Huberman.

Forget all about Devlin.

What can he offer you?

rock'n'rollero

Not that it matters, but my name is Carl. It's one of those names that never quite fit. I never seemed like much of a Carl once I'd reached puberty and my longest dearest closest friends and the four true loves of my life have never felt comfortable using the name. So one of the reasons I liked it at Marco's was that I had a nickname.

"Carlo!" Marco would greet me with his fake Italian accent, "What will you prepare tonight? How about that steak? The one with the salsa verde. I'm in the mood for beef tonight."

I was Carlo the Cook once I cinched on my apron over my white starched cook's shirt and picked up the ten-inch Wusthof, my chef's knife, full tang, the hardest steel the Germans could forge. This knife was ground by the ancient master in North Beach, the man with the paper bag hat. It has a deadly edge. Don't touch it. Only Gina can touch my chef's knife. Same goes for the twelve-inch slicer.

See? I have an entire personality now. My work persona. The times when I'm no longer Carl Carrasco bloodhoundin' for wine, women and song, but Carlo the Cook, self-proclaimed master of risotto and three pasta sauces I'll stand behind to the bitter end.

And with my persona comes a fluidity to Time. Work's the only time that Time runs right. The times I'm chopping away or shaking a sizzling sauté pan, watching the weather change out our back door. Forgetting for a moment.

I was the sous chef at Marco's. The second. This might have been more a career feather in my toque if we actually had customers and the kitchen staff numbered more than six (including me and the chef, Gina), but I *was* in charge on nights Gina wasn't around and I took my lording over the kitchen crew very seriously. Especially where Rock'n'Rollero was concerned.

It was Maxie that named Larry. I was bitching about Larry one day to Maxie in Spanish pretending Maxie cared and Maxie said, "Ahh, el Rock'n'Rollero." It was the perfect name.

Larry, our four-day-a-week grill cook, wasn't really a cook in the truest sense. He was less of a cook than myself since, in a sense, he was really a keyboardist. When he donned his checkers and whites it was only to pay the bills until he could finally whip his band into shape and conquer the music industry.

I, on the other hand, gained an identity when I donned my uniform. A reluctant one, but an identity nonetheless. While *my* free time had *less* definition, Rock'n'Rollero had a clear and brilliant vision of what he was outside of work. He was a flowing-haired rock star.

As Rock'n'Rollero's "boss," I had long ago dropped the notion of him ever picking up any cooking skills (or of us being any sort of friends) and my main goal was that he stop fucking the few waitresses we had while I went empty. Not that he fucked that many, it's just that I couldn't believe he fucked that one. The third waitress two before Moira.

If we were pals it would have been one thing. I might have at least slapped him on the back for the first coupla weeks until I was eventually green with the thought.

If we were pals, but Rock'n'Rollero simply didn't like me in the least. I tried to be nice at first and exercised none of my authority, but fuck it! If he couldn't be civil I'd order him around and watch the heat rise off his forehead and wonder whether he was man enough to actually quit or if he was all bluster. It started the day I mentioned he only cooked the polenta for ten minutes.

"What! Are you watching me?" He was immediately defensive, which immediately goads me on.

"Yeah, and you only cooked it for ten minutes."

"Oh, now you're the boss."

"I'm your boss on Sunday nights." I stared him right down. I had exerted my will, my superiority, because in the kitchen, unlike on the shores of philosophical debate, there is a hierarchy or the thing just won't really run. So, in the name of order and esprit de corps (and thanks to his initial unfriendliness to me, combined with him fucking that one third waitress and making ten-minute polenta) I had to finally tell Larry to stop fucking up and being a lazy cook. He didn't appreciate this at all and told me so (it was an under-the-breath "Fuck you" as he walked out of the kitchen for a moment, basically his last words to me).

Now on Sundays the silence between us drowns out the sound of the hood fans. I'd quit except that I like it here so I've dug in and am determined to show him who is Alpha Dog and who is Beta Bitch in the two-man weekday line at Marco's. Don't make me have to go to Gina! Maybe he did fuck that one third waitress but she's gone now and his band sucks and after tomorrow's lunch I'm off.

That's what work's like on Sunday.

phone call

I knew it was due. It had to be coming. The once-every-three-or-so-weeks phone call from . . . Her. You see, we're old enough and mature enough (at least . . . She is) to still remain "friends" despite our slightly bitter split-up. And we're friends in the most convenient sense of the word. The baker's dozen phone calls we'll make in this calendar year are enough for us to be able to answer with complete truth whenever an old acquaintance ever happens to ask, "So how's so and so doin'? You ever hear from her/him?" "Oh, yes!" we can truthfully testify. "He/She is doing fine. We just spoke on the phone last week."

See? That's much better than bursting into tears upon hearing their name mentioned or going into an unwanted (at least by the person you bump into on the street) tirade about what a mess it all was. This way I retain some dignity and might even pass myself off as a "together" kind of person.

The thing about the phone calls, though, is that they're so damn disconcerting. And I don't mean in the usual sense. In the first few weeks after the "divorce" the calls had a comforting predictable nature about them—screaming, accusations, weeping, lengthy silences, significant exhalations—but now that ten months have gone by and all the histrionics have become inappropriate we're left with nothing. I go blank and get tight whenever I hear her voice and it isn't from sad nostalgia or from truly missing her. It's the blankness itself that gets me tight. Like Oakland, there's no there there. She doesn't want me back and I don't want her back. I only want to want her back. And not her, really, for I've transformed . . . Her (**AIYEEHH!! AIYEEHH!!**) into a sort of Frankenstein's Daughter amalgam of the Ideal Woman (I go in more for the Loving/Abandoning Icon rather than the, in my opinion, more clichéd Madonna/Whore). So and so's sense of humor, another's easygoing nature, that woman's intelligence and taste, some nice eyes from column A, that great ass from column B and various images burned into my heart and mind from Hollywood movies of the forties to early sixties.

But then the phone rings.

K: Hey, what's up?

Me: Nothing . . . You?

K: Just thought I'd call.

Silence. I'm already a slightly uncooperative witness. I can't think of a thing to say (when in reality we can talk about a million things forever) so my brain begins to instantly compute the length of the ensuing silence to the nearest nanosecond.

K: Oh, did I tell you about my roommates? They've got more guests coming over this weekend.

M: Mmmm. . . .

K: Every weekend they've got somebody crashing out here.

M: That's no good.

K: So how's work?

M: Well, it seems Rock'n'Rollero has decided the doo-rag is the latest in aspiring rock star fashion.

She laughs.

K: Do you guys still not talk?

M: Oh, yeah. We don't talk all the time.

K: Guys.

   I take this personally.

M: How's your work?

K: Ach, it's so busy, but they gave me a promotion. Huh, it's quite a raise really.

M: Mmmm. . . . good (I'm so fucking happy that you now out-earn me). How are your parents?

K: Fine. My mom thinks she's going to get laid off.

M: She always thinks that. She thought that when we first met.

K: Yeah . . .

   Her voice trails off. That's how it goes. The chance reference to When We First Met skated dangerously close to the verboten topics: us, sex, dating and anything of an emotional nature. It was like the small talk When We First Met except back then we hoped things would get deeper and now we hope, instead, that they won't.

the breakup

As I hang up the phone I realize that the saving grace of the breakup, the silver lining in my darkest January, was the fact that not six weeks into the breakup, right around Valentine's Day (this provides me with an added satisfaction, that for once Valentine's Day actually worked to my advantage), the Other Guy broke up with . . . Her. Yeah, I didn't tell you before. I even lied to Mike.

"Is she fuckin' some other guy?" Mike asked me that first meeting after **Boom!** the year began.

"Uh, I don't think so." I couldn't say it.

"Is there some other guy?"

"Uh, maybe. I don't know."

"She's fuckin' him." Mike nodded like he was helping me out, ferreting out valuable information.

I knew. Right off. I looked at the phone transcripts. There were lots of calls to San Francisco. Well, about 67 to be exact. It worked out to 3.7 for every day beginning, according to Pac Bell records, two hours after my plane lifted off for Mexico City 'til a call that must have been made just before she jumped into the car to pick me up at the airport. Probably assuring him that she would not falter. That her resolve was true. That it was over. That she'd deliver the news.

She didn't seem quite right when she picked me up but as it unfolds before your eyes you hardly notice. I'd been gone a couple of weeks and she seemed a bit nervous, not her usual warm self. . . . Ah, maybe you're just being paranoid. But looking back you can now see the tiniest thing. A pause. The way she touches your hand. It all begins to make sense after the fact.

It was over. . . . She finally told me as we sat on the bed and I reached for her in that unmistakable way.

She pulled away with an angry look on her face that was replaced by an uncomfortable guilty look followed by a slowly constructed determined look while all the while I'm asking "What? What?"

The belated entrance of the Other Guy. I couldn't really comprehend it right off. It was supposed to be me that left. We'd nearly agreed on that point, but now with this other guy, with my fait accompli as fuel, the bed was practically spinning and I thought I might throw up for a moment.

And then Time slips back into place and in reality I'm sitting in my living room counting the minutes, to what I don't know. It's like I'm waiting out my life, and then I get angry. It's been over for ten months now but . . . She's still rousting about in my brain. A lost-love residue that 'causes minor malarial relapses. Love and Sex were killing me 'cause I was getting none of either.

ramona

Marco cherished the good review in the weekend food section we'd received back in September and he pinned it up in the window to lure in the occasional straggler that made it down to our end of the block. We had the food and Marco, ever full of hope, was the genial smiling host. He'd wear nice slacks and a fine Italian shirt, but never a sports coat. "What am I, at a funeral or some Mafia hit man?" he'd ask. "Maybe back East, but not in California."

Marco wanted to make Gina the star of his soon-to-be-wildly-successful restaurant, but Gina didn't know how to promote herself. She just didn't think it should be a part of the job. She was the chef; her realm was the kitchen; the cooks and dishwashers were her crew; the produce and fish and meats of the seasons were her raw material. She was never comfortable going out into the dining room and mingling with the customers unless it was a table of friends at the end of the night. To tell a table of regular customers how great the food was or to stand there while Marco introduced her as the amazing Chef Gina, from the Old World, magician with the food—she could barely smile through it all. "A cook's place is in the kitchen," she'd tell me. I liked that about her.

This was no end of frustration for Marco. He just knew he was missing out on a gold mine. "She's from Italy. Actually from Italy," he'd tell me during our slow lunches.

"I know," I'd say, for there was no denying that or what he was getting at, that we had this great chef with an accent that came from where the food originated.

But that didn't stop the rest of the week.

High Noon.

After the big-bust excitement of packed Friday and Saturday and a good rush from the notoriously finicky Sunday diners came at last the homestretch to my workweek. My two lunch shifts, when Marco's was transported from Oakland to Hadleyville. When Marco would stand by the cash register figuratively—and sometimes actually—wringing his hands at the lack of money going into it. Other times he would simply stare into it as though in a trance or waiting for some sign from above as far as what to do next.

I stand behind the stove fully at the ready. Practically daring an order to come in, my ear cocked for the faint ring of the front door bell. Nothing. No one comes in. Our end of the avenue sits dead and lifeless. Only Gary Cooper could possibly be walking down that deserted street waiting for the train bearing the Miller Boys' hopes for vengeance. That's no kind of an atmosphere for lunch and so we sit in a quiet, nearly empty restaurant.

I loved it at first, money for nothing. I'd prepare the night's specials in the calm comfortable air of all the time in the world, simply cooking in the light of day, an occasional pasta or focaccia sandwich order, eating two full meals (not counting the 24/7 light grazing), fantasizing on Niko and pussy in general, waiting to head the half-block north to Jacko's for the first pint. But after a while Marco's suffering began cutting into my enjoyment of the easy life.

As the weeks of slow weekday business progressed (Marco feared the coming winter as badly as I) I could almost hear his anguish above the humming hoods as he fretted over the lack of business.

Niko's making a vinaigrette, telling me: "That's right. I beat up Danny Glover's youngest daughter. With a stick! Oooh, he was mad. They used to live two doors down. Before he got all big and shit, don't talk to no one like me anymore, hih-hih-hih," she laughs. "Yeah, that was before he got famous. But I whipped that li'l girl's *ass*." Niko smiles broadly, pleased as punch. "Talkin' shit?!? Excuse me?"

Outside not a soul stirred. Life stopped four blocks short and Marco sometimes just couldn't resist. Even though he knew better, he'd step outside and look longingly north up the Avenue. You could see it, the traffic and pedestrians. All the bustle of commerce just a few short blocks but worlds away.

Ding!

"Three blocks! Three blocks further north and we'd have trouble keeping up with the business," he'd announce as he stepped back inside. If it was after two he'd have his first glass of wine.

Into this vacuum stepped Ramona, our steady-as-a-rock lunch waitress, who transformed Marco's Trattoria into Ramona's Restaurant. She was our very own New Age, postmodern hippie waitress, complete with unsolicited aura reviews and essential cellular salts that she carried on her person at all times. Ramona cruised the weekday lunch floor performing extreme New Age philosophizing and prescribing while waiting tables.

Ramona was in the process of becoming a certified healer and our sixteen to twenty-four lunch customers were some of her first clients. She even offered to "heal" me for free. Today, for instance, in the heat of the lunch rush (which meant eleven people were in the restaurant all at the same time), Ramona busted out for all to hear,

"Have you been using dairy again?

"Huh?" She'd caught me off guard again. "What makes you think I ever stopped? 'Cause you claim cows are evil?"

"Milk is for babies. What you need is a woman."

"What?!" I couldn't be sure she had said it, or at least I couldn't believe she said it that way. Like "Take care of your simple shit." I had to ask. "You talkin' to me?"

"And I don't mean a fuck," she added, and walked out of the kitchen carrying a Parma ham sandwich and a hot coppa pizzetta for table six.

Niko pretended to be lost in her now *very* careful stacking of romaine lettuce leaves for a ceasar salad. I could see the big smile she was trying so hard to contain.

"What? What's so funny?"

"Huh?" Niko asked all serious. "You talking to me?"

"Yeah."

Ramona was back. "I know this really great chiropractor . . ."

"What?! I thought I need a woman." Niko couldn't keep from laughing so she excused herself on some pretense of getting supplies.

"I can see from here your meridians are all out of alignment."

"I really don't . . ." I didn't know what the fuck Ramona was talking about. She was so free and loose with the New Age Magical Mystery paradigm from which she operated. It was practically wanton.

"You're resisting." Ramona's brow was furrowed as she "examined" me. "I can see it from here. I'm picking up anxious unsettled energy about you. You need to relax more. Look at your posture."

My posture was never the greatest, but I had to ask, "Don't you have any tables out there? Aren't there diners dropping off chairs from hunger by now? Cash register being rifled?"

Ramona looked at me with that tender mournfulness reserved for lost souls. "Sad clown," she said, and left with a couple of salads.

The doors swung open after a few minutes. "Hold your hand out. Come on, it's red algae—a very potent cell detoxificant."

"Ramona . . ."

"Oh, and I have this special order." She handed me the tag.

"A spirulina pesto pasta?!" Ramona liked to place orders for things we didn't have. She'd just invent it as she went along and give me a list of ingredients. "Ramona, we don't have spirulina pesto."

"Just take the cheese out of the pesto. I have the spirulina right here."

"You can't take the cheese out. It's blended. The cheese is completely blended in."

"You can't take the cheese out?"

"A centrifuge couldn't take the cheese out."

That's when Marco would stick his head in the door and say in that steady firm voice he used when he wanted people to know he was really being serious now,

"Ramona," motioning for the dining room, but it was Gina's day off, so the muscle was gone and, besides, about a third of the people in the dining room were friends of Ramona's or people who came in for the highly recommended vegetarian and even vegan dishes she'd invent. I perfected ratatouille under her encouragement.

Ramona was overflowing with an extra helping of nurture lately owing to the fact that she'd recently fallen head over heels in love with . . . some guy. A leprechaun actually. Well, not that I believe he sprang to life from a box of cereal. It was Ramona who claimed this. Or that he had once been a leprechaun in a previous incarnation. Or possessed a leprechaun energy. I can't remember exactly because I don't care. I did meet him once and there was no denying that an air of leprechuanness hung about him. He was maybe five-two, red hair, upturned little nose, clear blue eyes, freckly. He didn't have the bowler, but he *had* written a new jingle for a bug extermination company.

"And the bastards? They ripped me off! Robbed me of my rightful royalties."

Well, top o' the mornin' to ya, I'm thinking. Who is this guy?

Ramona made the introductions and quietly wondered if I could front him a sandwich. Red Green was his name. They made a weird but somehow right couple. Like maybe there was something to it after all.

jane

And then there was Jane. Could there be a more plain name than Jane? And for such an exotic creature? You could tell from the start that it was probably a go and she actually laughed and had me that quickly sworn off Russian women.

Forget these Warsaw Pact intellectuals. I decided to go blue collar soon after meeting Jane at this bar I never go to, stumbled into by chance really, looking for Mike who was nowhere to be found. It's Wednesday, my Big Time Saturday Night when I've earned my drink. Mike never showed probably 'cause his woman wouldn't let him leave the house so I started talking to the bartender at this place down in Oakland, a town which has stuck away in it all sorts of tiny lost Oaktown corners great neighborhood bars coated with a patina of ancient character.

Jane.

Jane Kolchak.

It was near closing and Jane, either not caring about or not noticing my DUI state, asked if I might give her a ride home.

"Of course!" I told her, and "Of course!" my mind told me. A blue-collar girl and a bartender to boot. What could be more natural? Me and a bartender. Free beer and sex might soon be mine.

And so it was that Jane waltzed into my life and into my bedroom, saving me momentarily from . . . Her.

Jane Kolchak. Five-nine with the most lovely long limbs and easy laugh. Both her parents are Slovakian, born in the Old World, you know. I'm on some sort of Behind the Iron Curtain run here. Anastasia has whetted my appetite and now I'm onto a second-generation fellow American version.

It took a bit of doing which included a specific back-off warning on Date Three with her claiming I had pressed the matter too far on Date Two, but she's new to California and has fallen head over heels for October. We're in our shirt sleeves enjoying a warm sunny day at the lake and she doesn't realize what's coming. She doesn't see the urgency. Time, you know.

The back-off warning took place upon a park bench at Lake Chabot, where swam fat, elusive bass. It's a beautiful lake that looked more like the lakes of my SoCal homeland. Jane wanted to make grilled vegetables and snapper and we had cold beers in the cooler and I liked that about her, that she was cool and easy, a beer-drinking girl from the North Shore. She had a Midwestern accent and a kielbasas-and-taverns look about her dressed up in macho dyke clothing with a bit of an attitude (I'd stepped into a big pile of . . . sassy!).

Here was a girl with a motorcycle who worked as a bartender and was just beginning to dabble in bisexuality. A modern miracle of safely kinky sex lay within my grasp. I could hardly contain myself.

We were sippin' beer at the lake picnic table watching a bunch of Latino kids running and playing, the BBQ going and by some freak chance the Russian girl came by with some geek and her Russian mother whom I said hello to. It seemed like I had women all over the place, like they couldn't even help but bump into each other, and yet I wasn't gettin' a dang thing. I was still outta the dang saddle, boy!

After the back-off warning at the Lake Chabot picnic grounds, Date Four had a comfortable measured pace to it with a little decorum and restraint as far as the breast fondling and tongue plunging were concerned. We then both—in an unspoken agreement—doubled the alcohol consumption on Date Five when she at last gave herself up to me. One date too late for me, but within reason and I couldn't figure the reason because Jane was one of those girls who just came alive on a bed. She'd excuse herself and don tights and leggings, lacy bras, she'd practically bubble in the candlelight.

I was back in the saddle! and any sex hunger or love hunger or horniness's lonely pain or heart's deep endless ache were instantly gone. I'm that simple at times.

work

I came to work the next morning with my Johnny Cash CD, a big grin pasted on my face and the smell of her on my hand. Jane. The new girl. The fourth after . . . Her (Grrrr!) and the memory of last night and a whiff of my hand like some sort of breakup and loneliness decongestant made me feel amazingly great though I'd hardly slept.

Johnny was singing about jails and women and hard times and I saw how silly my funk had been. Back in the saddle felt good.

"What the fuck you listenin' to?" Niko came in like she thought I'd gone mad. "What's this hillbilly shit?"

"It's Johnny Cash, man."

"More like Johnny Trash. Johnny White Trash." Niko began to heat her pot of milk and I continued some peaceful prep work at the table. Through the door you could see a tree and you'd get glimpses of the outside that spoke of freedom—the glance of sunlight, the squabbling of tiny birds. It could be so beautiful.

"Oh, now what? I don't believe it," Niko dropped her wooden spoon into her pot of warming milk. "You did. The white boy finally got him some. Yeah."

"What?!" I smiled.

"Look at you. Shit. Somebody finally fucked his brains out," and then she turned away and yelled, "Hey! Everybody can calm down now. White Boy got some."

"Oh, I'm not that bad."

"Hey, Max!" Niko turned to me, "Is Max in yet?"

"Yeah, I think he's out back sweeping."

"Now, how you say that?" she asked me. "Calmate? Yeah. Hey, Max! Calmate your ass today. Mister Carlos is all happy now. Probably do all his own prep today. Probably peel garlic even."

all-night pharmacy

So I'm at the all-night pharmacy store. It's not exactly all-night, but it's open 'til eleven, which is as close as it gets here and I'm on a mission involving my teeth and my penis (I'm now the swingin' kind of stud who requires fresh condoms late at night).

I was in the market for some sort of miracle stop-the-stabbing-throbbing-of-a-back-molar (do not ever let any liquid less than 52 degrees touch that molar unless you want your entire universe pinpointed on that screaming tooth) ointment and the thinnest condom that exists in the Western World.

On the way back to the checkout one of those filled "pies"—chocolate, berry, whatever; the kind stacked up in a display thing delivered by the semiload from "bakeries" I cannot even conceptualize right then—catches my eye so I grab a "chocolate" one and I'm next up in line for the tall young male cashier with the shaved-head-'cept-for-green-forelock look (and I'm pleased with my local pharmacy for recognizing my community's standards).

I can't fucking wait. I'm gonna slather that fucking entire back upper left molar region with this shit and for Jane—ooh Jane—waiting back in bed I got the condoms and a Kern's apricot nectar (she'll be so happy when I deliver this beverage to her, she doesn't even have to get up). Plus there's the pie for the walk back!

But then there's a problem with the scanner and a red-handed customs moment begins to take place as the green-hair-forelocked checker leans the gooseneck-mounted mike toward him and announces over the entire store loudspeaker system,

"Price check on Cank-Aid, extra-strength. Can I get a price check on Cank-Aid? That's the extra-strength, family-sized for cankers and cold sores. Price check please . . . Cank-Aid."

I look down at my meager purchase and for the first time notice that my tooth ointment screams from its cardboard packaging "**CANKER SORES**" and I'm instantly reduced to cankerous scum requiring extra sensitivity in my condoms and soothing salves for my gigantic mouth sores, unable to resist the completely artificial "chocolate" "pie."

"Huh." The cashier kind of laughs and I can feel myself redden. "These pies are great. We get 'em forty percent off."

I was immensely relieved. "What's that make 'em? Twenty cents each?"

"I don't know," the guy said, "But two dollars buys plenty of 'em."

"Cool."

Back home I could hardly believe it. There she was. Jane. Right on the bed even. She's got on this tight bodysuit that has the perfect cut. It makes her legs look endless.

"Oooh, you got me a Kern's!" She seems so nice and happy about this little thing that I've done.

The room was lit yellow. It was a nice room all of a sudden. What had been my empty prison was now softly lit, with a girl who's so pleased to be sipping an apricot nectar, but I barely notice any of that because I'm nuzzling her neck. That's my sweet nectar right now, leaning into her breasts, my wet hungry mouth open.

"Let's go to bed," she says, and this makes her the greatest thing in my entire life right then.

She's on the bed, on all fours, the top of her bodysuit pulled down off her shoulders, her soft peach skin exposed, the ripe swell of her breasts rising with each breath.

Right then, at this great moment of sheer desire, I begin to mentally confirm the location of the freshly bought condoms and how and when they will come into play.

But her thighs! They were wonderment as we both fell back onto the covers. These long shapely legs were firm and lean yet soft as could be as I ran the palms of my hands up the length of them, toward the little spot that I dreamt of, that little sweet honey pot. Beyond the thin veil of her leotard lay the sucking wet, liquid warmth. The stuff dreams are made of.

This slippery bliss engulfed my middle finger as I slipped it into Jane, who gasped satisfyingly from deep within her throat. That's when I made the mistake of monitoring the progress of my cock. It was gorging nicely, but I began to fret again the tricky Condom Retrieval/Slapping On Process systems.

Oh, the moves I've got pretty much mapped out after ten months of single life. I have the Condom Drill down, but no matter what, it always quickly deteriorates into a frantic game of Beat the Clock.

The declaration of The Moment when the surgery room material comes out. The tearing open of The Package. They never just open. Not like a beer. It's like the wrapping on a CD! You can't get the shit open! Already time is being lost. The moment fades ever so slightly, the cock senses that something is up. It begins the first hints of curling up and hiding. And then at last! Out comes the condom like a proctologist late for his appointment, but which way does it roll?! You never know. It's like 50-50. "They can put a man on the moon . . . ," I could hear my old man complain. No! Not Dad! Don't think of Dad at the same time cocks and pussies are flying about your brain! This grievous mental error immediately drained twenty percent of the blood out of my cock, leaving it good for most fuckings, but questionable when it came to the penetration of the condom, which gives up its full form as easily as a tense, slim-hipped virgin.

I finally figured out which way the fucker unrolled. I felt its cold grip on the tip, the tip! The attempt at roll-down had begun. The deadening feel of latex. I was losing it.

"What's the matter?" Jane asked as she lay on her back, her legs spread and her pussy in full wet bloom.

"Uh . . . nothing, heh!" I could feel my existence expand rapidly, the heat on the back of the neck. I was in the opening stages of Red Alert Performance Anxiety and could feel the blood rush into my face when it was supposed to be going the other direction.

"I know, you want me to suck your cock, huh?" She smiled and swung around to face me. In an instant she was on her haunches, three-quarters of it in the moist paradise of her mouth, and suddenly I knew all was right with the world. No matter what, I thought, I can now die a happy man.

camping with jane

They warned me. Mike came right out and yelled, "What are you thinking?!" while Marco just quietly stated, "It's a little soon . . . ," but the weather was poised to turn and she wanted to go camping and I kept picturing her in those tights and I thought this camping adventure might glue her to me enough to cover the entire winter up to Valentine's Day, when any hope I had of maintaining whatever relationship I might at that time have found myself in was thrown out the window.

They were right. That food poisoning I suffered fifty miles down the road from a chance bad San Rafael burrito is a picnic in my mind right now as I stare at the steering wheel of my car, far too uptight to look directly at the near-black cloud up ahead. It's looking especially threatening from the vantage point of a heavily rutted dirt road.

"I think we need to go a little farther." Jane looks up from a map that for some reason she's consulting sideways so that the state of California now runs east to west. Even ignoring the condition of her cardinal points, the state map is not nearly detailed enough for our predicament. It doesn't even begin to address the tampering of sensitive pyschosexual relationship orbitals by camping, let alone depict any sort of small county nonmaintained dirt road.

All I know is that we're twenty-three miles in, four forks deep, winding our way, supposedly, down to a lake at the far end of the Eel River, one of the few rivers that run from south to north (the Nile and Rhine being the most famous) except that according to Jane's map, the Eel now runs from east to west.

Compounding matters is a black cloud up ahead that I'm fairly certain is the front line of that hundred-year stormy season they've been forecasting for the last six months. This is not looking good.

"Maybe we should have gone right on that last one." Her brow is furrowed and she has that sweet worried look on her face that four forks deep I no longer find so sweet.

"I really think we should head back," I say for the millionth time. It's pretty much all I've said the past long, slow nine miles, each switchback convincing me that much more that this, too, will not result in the love-packed or even holiday-ride-out relationship I've sort of been hoping for.

The Monster . . . She I see now in a golden flattering light. . . . She likes to come out whenever the new girls let me down again. And while . . . She remains a monster, the black cloud ahead bathes her in light soft and delicate. It brings out her finely arched eyebrows, the natural brownness of her skin, her black eyes.

AIYEEEH!! AIYEEEH!!

I know I shouldn't indulge myself. It works better to imagine that . . . She does not exist, rather than to picture her in nostalgia's finery. To imagine her life cut tragically short is more comforting (as far as *my* mental health goes). I even have a fitting scenario worked out for her new San Francisco hip and trendy persona. Blowfish. The famed but potentially deadly culinary delight. Finest of all the sushi. The most highly prized.

Woman Dies Of Sushi Blowfish Poisoning,
the headline screams in the Chronicle.

"That's terrible," beautiful female friends console me (this part is also made up. I have no beautiful female friends and not that many male friends, beautiful or not).

"I know." I shake my head, staring at the ground, and then look up at them through the tears. "I ordered the bonito."

A hot clingy-cocktail-dress-clad woman gives me a hug and whispers in my ear, "I love the bonito, too."

"If we just go a little farther down this way . . . ," Jane says.

I was back in my skin, in real time, still stuck in a car on a dirt road with a bisexual who has yet to produce a threesome. I'm certain that however far we get, by daybreak the way back will be impassable mud. We'll be stranded in the farthest reaches of the Mendocino National Forest living off rainwater collected in old shoes. Once our overly-stocked-in-snacks-and-beverages supplies run out we'll be rationing the two six-month-old Power Bars found in the car's toolbox, a threesome completely out of the question.

"It's probably just ahead." Jane tries to say it in a positive helpful way. She's one of those people who are most positive except when things aren't going just right. There's a certain fragility to her hopefulness.

"I think we should head back," I try to break reality to her in a most gentle manner. "That cloud . . ."

Jane looked up from her map and gave me this look like she's worried about whether the boys are gonna make it back home from overseas. I don't know why she would look at me with such a look but that's what it looked like to me. I was threatening, in a distant far-off sort of way, to the very fabric of her life. I just wasn't the big burly kind of broad-shouldered man that could make her world safe for sporadic-bisexual-encounter monogamy. "Just a little farther . . ."

"What about El Niño?! Huh?" I finally bust.

"You're so pessimistic. I can't deal with pessimism."

She thinks we need to go farther. I think we've gone too far and are hopelessly lost. We have the same views concerning our "relationship."

When we met, or more accurately, once consummation took place, she told me of her love of freedom, her need for a girl once in a while. She spoke of an open relationship. One where we could both go out and see other women and maybe bring them home. I'm thinking, Yeah! Fuckin' yeah!! He shoots, he scores! I be bad. . . . She dries up and shrivels to nothing faster than Margaret Hamilton in Oz.

Needless to say, the bisexual orgies starring me, Jane and (I keep my fantasies realistic in the hopes that this will somehow encourage their realization) an occasional plain woman and, once in a great while, a superhot one, had yet to materialize.

It truly was a fantasy in the end. Jane wanted more, more than I could deliver so soon after . . . Her (**AIYEEEH!! AIYEEEH!!**) Same as her camping plans (deeper and deeper in we had to go) Jane was never satisfied and I inadvertently (or not, maybe) blew it later that night in the tent as a light rain fell outside making it quite cozy inside with her. Before we went to sleep she said she loved me. Not that she was in love with me, but that she loved me and she just wanted to say that and it was rather touching, really. She was shy and sweet about it, too. A hidden softness 'cause Jane liked to seem tough in her leather and boots.

I'm not sure what I mumbled or maybe I merely smiled weakly in the dark, but I silently balked. The proclamation or the lie, "I love you" stuck in my craw. I was neither a good boyfriend nor a true scoundrel.

I mean, we were sitting in the forest, our tent pitched, huddled inside, the rain lightly falling outside and she was good to go when we went. That was the greatest thing of all about Jane, good and lively in bed. And she even played a tape of Hendrix that some pal from back in her taverns land had made for her and the music was great and what more could I want? The timing was perfect, the first rains of the year and my cupboard is now stocked. I'm inside a dry tent with a warm girl. But it just wasn't perfect. It just wasn't.

The problem was that the last thing on my mind was love. A good ten months after . . . Her (**Whih-CACK!!** I snap my whip out at the beast, stinging her thigh, subduing her for a moment), I still wasn't in the mood for Love. Love was not a many-splendored thing and I felt more like Joe Gillis in *Sunset Boulevard* than Mark Elliot. I still could have nothing to do with Love.

But, it's been ten months! you're thinking. *How long do you fucking need? How long exactly were you and . . . She together?* I answer, Does it matter? What if I said it was five years? What if I said three months? What if it was only a few nights, would any of my responses necessarily convey the depth, the intensity and profundity of the affair?

Sure, it's all in the past now and that's what's important. That it's over. But for some reason there remains in my heart some sick longing, some twisted vision. It's branded upon my brain and does not allow me to even pretend to love sweet Jane snug with me inside a tent, dry from the rain, deep in the Mendocino National Forest listening to Jimi. So it was obviously long enough.

time

Time slipped another cog today. It's been doing that lately. Along with the rapid expansion and contraction of my existence, Time's clutch problems are nearly disturbing except that for the most part I observe all with the detached disdain of a bored monarch.

But Time was getting completely out of hand. It might happen at any time, Time's clunky flow. When Time became a Changeling and it was difficult to imagine what time it was exactly. Was it the seventies or the nineties? Is that nineteen-year-old in tie-dye not time-transported here from the late sixties? He bears all the trappings. And that crew-cutted man in his thirties wearing horn-rimmed glasses. Didn't I see him in that footage of Governor Wallace and the attack dogs?

And then there was Jane. The thing with Jane—for my male psyche to operate in an upright fashion on the streets my brain has rereleased it as *The Jane Incident* starring William Holden in one of his slightly uncomfortable-fitting roles as the romantic leading man—had lasted a total of seventeen days and this included a camping trip.

That was unheard of. Typically, short relationships involving travel were measured in months. It has to be El Niño. Time's Accelerator caught momentarily and

SNAP!

Outta the saddle and now it's winter. There's no denying tonight's storm. The night the rains came. The first big storm of the
year. The Child knocks. El Niño sitting its fat ass off the coast, a
big warm pool of water twice the size of the continental U.S. driving systems we can only guess at, sending my puny existence spinning madly about, making one hour take a lifetime while another
week passes in the blink of an eye.

Tonight I came to at the Pho shop. The girl brings me a steaming bowl. Apparently I've already ordered. It's some sort of joke. I
can get a meal that is both a culinary event and most of the food
I'll need for the day for $4.75. It ranks up there with the machaca
plate down on University Avenue or the Chaat House.

I'm sitting before this large steaming bowl of Pho and while the
change of the season from the dry and warm and long of day to the
wet and cold and long of night carries with it an added coldness
due to lack of squeeze, I feel enlivened by my steaming bowl of
soup. In its light fragrant broth thin slices of beef sit atop a hidden
boiling hot iceberg of noodles. Floating green rafts of jalapeños
promise me tastebudular excitement. I throw in some torn-off cilantro leaves, bean sprouts and a healthy squeeze of lime and have
at it.

The promise is realized and between slurping gulps of the soup
I eye the Vietnamese girl taking orders tonight. She's a beauty and
with her and my video and the rain coming and my Pho I'm in
heaven. It's but three blocks home and I've got *The Rise and Fall
of the Roman Empire*. I deeply lament the fact that *Boy on a Dolphin*
is not available on video and Stephen Boyd's plastic-faced Livius *is*
a bit bothersome, but the glorious letter-boxed version in Ultra
Panavision 70 is just big enough to contain the most amazing pair
of eyes in cinema history. Those dark bewitching Sophia Loren orbs.

I sit on my couch deeply in love. My belly is full of Pho and

I'm truly, regretfully (hitting playback and pause at just the right moment as she fills the screen, my TV, my heart) in love with Sophia Loren.

They're all gone again. All the women. All I have is this drawer next to my desk. It has a few cards in it. Little love notes handwritten by a few girls I used to know. They say how glad they were we met. How happy they are. How they look eagerly forward to times ahead. They express happiness and gratification and, even, in rare instances, love, but they're all gone tonight. All I have is Sophia and these cards.

The latest layer has been added to . . . Her. The very faint Jane Strata. You see, . . . She has become more than any one woman. . . . She has become a sad, sick idealized amalgam. . . . She has become my few true loves and K—— and Ingrid and that girl I should have grabbed way back when in college and dark beautiful Maria and now Jane. And tonight an extra helping of Sophia as the beautiful Lucilla.

gina's sister

The very next day I'm back at work and in walks a smaller and much less voluptuous come-to-life version of Sophia Loren herself who turns out to be the famous sister of Gina who Marco had mentioned to me in whispered tones even though Gina wasn't even in the restaurant at the time.

I fell completely in love with her the moment she walked through the kitchen with a little smile and extra juice.

I've actually engaged with three of this type of woman in my entire life. The kind you instantly fall for. All to disastrous effect. Broken hearts, maxed-out credit cards, needlessly-worried-over trips to the free clinic where the first glimpse of the netherworld of sub-middle-class-standard life awaits you. It seems most people my age have given in by now and paid their very own doctors fifty bucks for the test, but I persevere.

Gina introduces me to her sister, Daniela. She looks a lot like Gina except her face is less fleshy. And her hair. It's endless. It's even blacker than Gina's maybe and wound into some bun tail. I imagine it might stretch down to the small of her back which I'll bet is olive-skinned and flawless with fine downy hairs.

She's got this electric neon blue eye shadow that looks slutty hot. Daniela's got that subtle bit of tramp about her that I always look for, but I don't dare to approach the company of Gina's very own sister. Family, you know. Plus I get the impression that there's a wee bit o' sisterly rivalry going on. Gina takes her for the irresponsible one, trading on her looks. Daniela plays up her youth and beauty. She's a natural for the role. The pretty one. She's always been the pretty one and Gina the talented one. They have to have roles, right?

The next night it was Marco out front and Gina at home and Marco and I are eating a slice of fritatta when I mention to him that I had seen Daniela.

"Ahh, Daniela, la piccola sorella." He had a look and I was sure we were both bonded on our fuck desire for her. "Table twelve!" He marched out of the kitchen and not another word was ever spoken of little Daniela.

nurse!

As I headed home Daniela had me all fired up and Jane was freshly gone and I was almost tempted to call,

Nurse!

Nurse! was the woman I was "dating" before Jane finally stumbled into my life for seventeen days and since she's the last one before Jane who's actually slept with me . . . Well, I'm really tempted to call her up. But *I* broke up with *her*!

And it's not like we had some great thing going. I realize, in retrospect, which is the best vantage point for me, that I had fallen for Nurse! on the basis of A) She was good to go, peeling down to panties on the second date, promising great nastiness to come, B) She lived in a part of town where both parking and commuting posed no great problem and C) a vague fantasy of mine involving free medical attention and possibly some fun prescription medicine I was sure all nurses carried in their purses or had lying about the back of their kitchen drawers.

I don't know, now that Jane's gone I wonder if maybe I shouldn't have told Nurse! to go and fuck herself. You know, try and keep her in the stable. Have Nurse! as the charter member of my dreamt-of harem. But I was a wild man back then and had been on a good streak and just dumped her ass reveling in my scoundrelish nature. If only I had known.

At the time I even thought I'd finally figured out the proper way to end a . . . relationship—engtanglement? Whatever you want to call it (and since this one could be measured in weeks, "relationship" is a bit of a stretch)—do it quickly. Preferably over the phone.

Ah, Nurse! I can't call you. As much as I might be tempted (it's cold and windy on my walk home). All you'd have to do is laugh in my face (in my face over the phone, it works as well as in your face in person) and hang up and I've lost. There go all the points I've garnered for telling you to go fuck yourself and hanging up on *you*.

So instead Time slips once more and for the last few blocks to my house (when my has-no-woman status will be confirmed for the night) I'm back in her apartment.

It sat at the end of a very long hallway that was always dead quiet. Only Nurse! standing at the end of it after she buzzed me in. She'd be standing at the end of that long hallway always with a smile and a quick peck and a pat on the back. She takes my coat and tells me to wash up, she's got dinner ready.

I take a shower to rinse off the sticky sweat of work and revel again in the great pleasure of showering in a woman's bathroom. They're always so fresh and white with fluffy towels a good three times thicker and softer than the ones men manage and the soap is always hair-free.

She would make me dinner and the two of us would sit together at the table (she liked to watch me eat and took pleasure in feeding me). I'd be drinking some crappy Millers she usually had in the fridge for me.

"I can tell most of the time. Which ones are going to die." Nurse! said this just as I wolfed another slice of the pork chop

baked in a glass dish with tomatoey stuff on top. It was quite good.
"I can."

"Really?" I had to say something.

"Yeah, they have a look in their eye. Like they're ready, or sometimes the scared ones."

"Mmmm, that would be creepy." The hour would now be far
later and the night way more quiet and I'd have a flash in my mind
that she might poison me or kill me in my sleep.

"It's a lot of responsibility for her."

"For who?"

"A nurse!"

"Oh . . . Pork chop's good."

"You want another?" she would ask, now a smiling happy Betty
Crocker persona, far removed from the Night Shift Angel of Death
role I'd just seen her in.

Needless to say, after the sex it'd be another tossing-and-turning
night. I'd keep trying to catch her peeking at me out of the corner
of her eye, pretending to be asleep, patiently waiting for me to nod
off and then!

Well, I'm not sure what, but something really bad. I knew I
shouldn't have pursued it when she told me how her husband left
her but then she'd tell me "I like to be bad" or "This girl's nasty."
Stuff like that makes one forget. You can lose your head when all
the blood rushes to the other one.

So we slipped almost instantly into a nineties dating/domesticity
arrangement. Me the single man with crappy job and rented flat,
she the single mother with reluctantly supportive ex-husband and
slightly out-of-control young boy. I'd drop by after work (two times
a week was my max) and we'd sit and watch some inane sitcom
(she liked quite a few of them). She'd bitch about her job, I'd bitch
about mine, her kid would go hyper at some point (Vasectomy,
Vasectomy, my brain lobbied) and then she'd yell at him. I'd be

sitting trying to get into *Ellen,* making cricket sounds with a mostly empty MGD can.

Thankfully there was bed and Nurse! had a tight little body and occasionally she would bust out with some nasty bedroom tricks (this is why I'm tempted to call her up). It was all right. We'd do the nasty and then, spent, Nurse! would turn away and fall asleep almost instantly, right next to me. She felt nice leaning her small backside against my stomach, that annoying streetlight shining through her venetian blinds, me usually frustrated as hell.

Nurse! was the only woman I ever dated who would have her fun—throw her load, so to speak—and then roll over on her side and go to sleep. It didn't matter where I was in the matter. I could be hanging on the very edge, mere strokes away from sweet ecstasy. So fucking what?! seemed to be her attitude. She even told me once, "Hey, once this girl gets off, she's done."

Nurse! often referred to herself in the third person or as "this girl" and usually with a tough guy attitude like I better not get any ideas about fucking with her.

On the plus side, she did allow me to grind away inside of her for a bit more if I could get it back in. But after about three minutes of that she'd turn around, punch me in the sternum with the side of a closed fist and yell, "Hey! This girl's trying to get some sleep!"

Looking back, I think more than her often punching me in the chest, what finally put an end to it was the heater (that and her mysteriously vanishing 45 percent of the times we had arranged to get together. It was always some spur of the moment skiing trip or a flight to Vegas with her never-loses-at-the-casinos mom). But the heater?! She had that thing cranked to the point that whenever I did finally somehow will myself into a feverish sleep my dreams were hellish desert experiences with bizarre cameos by Peter

O'Toole and Omar Sharif. I took to bringing jugs of water and moist towelettes bedside in an effort to get through the night.

The first three or four times I spent the night with Nurse! I was convinced I was coming down with something (lying there, awake, cooking in the heat, making sure she's not gonna kill me, wondering, Why *did* her husband leave her in the middle of the night while she was on her death watch shift? According to her, he somehow packed up the entire belongings of a three-bedroom house, loaded them into a U-Haul and drove off with the good car in the matter of a few hours. It just doesn't add up and now he wants her back, of course. Beggin' and cryin', whinin' like a little bee-yach, hmmm . . .). Finally, I smuggled a thermometer in my night bag (it's a four-by-six-inch bag with hairbrush, toothbrush, condoms, lubes, dental floss and, you never know when it might come in handy—a tiny flashlight) and confirmed that I wasn't suffering from pre-AIDS night sweats. It was seventy-four degrees in the bedroom!

"Are you insane?!" I asked her as I flashed the thermometer before her.

"I can't believe you brought a thermometer with you." She wore a disappointed look.

"Well, I don't think it's healthy to have it so hot when you're sleeping," I argued.

"Hey, this girl likes it warm and comfy at night."

"But it's not comfy. It's like the fucking desert!"

Nurse! then tried to claim that the climate for the entire three-story apartment building was set by the never-seen manager in some sort of mythical apartment he supposedly lived in on the top floor. It seems the tenants had no control over their own destiny as far as temperature went.

"You mean to tell me you can't even turn down the heat if you wanted to?" I asked angrily. It was our first "fight." A near-bonding experience for the new couple that I can barely stomach. Making up is only good with someone you actually care about.

"Yeah, that's what I'm saying." She shot me her tough guy look and brandished a fist at me. "If this girl could control the thermostat, she would have by now."

Two weeks later I made the fateful call. Once again she'd been nowhere to be found at 8 P.M. the night before when we had specifically made plans to get together at 8 P.M. I decided to ask Mike for some advice. Though I doubted his claim to be something of an expert on women, he *was* now living with Kat rent-free, and well, that was good enough for me.

"Tell her to go fuck herself," was what Mike told me.

"That's your advice?! I can't just come out and say that," I protested.

"Why not? Are you guys getting along?"

"Ahh, not really."

"Okay then. Tell her to go fuck herself. It'll be over in a second."

"I don't know . . . ," I hesitated.

"Dump her fuckin' ass. *Fuck* her!" Mike was pissed off at Nurse! even though they'd never even met. "I mean, why bother? It'll be like laser amputation compared to gnawing your paw off in some fuckin' Yukon blizzard like you did the last time."

Ouch! My brain smarted at that one. "Fuck her!" I exclaimed loudly.

"Hell yes! Fuck her!"

"But I should go for sex one more time. I say fuck her one more time and then tell her, 'Fuck you!' "

"Exactly. Now you're talkin'," Mike agreed. "The only other option is to suggest a threesome."

"What's that?"

"The backup plan's telling her to go fuck herself after you fuck her one more time."

"The three-way . . ." I stroked my chin as I pondered Mike's relationship advice. He *was* persuasive.

"Yeah, what do you have to lose?" he asked.

As it turned out, the option of having sex with someone other than my hand.

clutch bunny and tha dogg

It's a day off and Mike and I are gonna go visit this friend who's maybe losing his fucking mind. Somehow Kat isn't along for the ride. Class or something (she was one of those late-twenties perma-students). We're on our way to see Tha Dogg, who, before El Niño, was known to everybody as Randall.

Jane was still sour on my mind and this made me think of Maria who was still sour on my mind and I didn't dare think about K—— who was beyond sour in my mind so I settled into this fantasy involving me on a warm beach with Sophia Loren, circa 1958.

Mikey is once again bitching about Kat, how he's fairly certain she followed him (I assure him the word he wants is "stalked") to a movie he went to with Neil and for some reason while he gets to bitch all day about his woman and how he has to give tons of emotional support (which for most men amounts to more than three consecutive minutes of any sort of caring) and how she won't let him do anything and he has to deal with all sorts of crap, I can't even bring up my sourness on women because I'm single. If I gripe at all I sound like some wimp ass wuss.

Once again the Bachelor Duo is foiled. It was kind of a drag. If I'm, say, Robin, lookin' to score, cruisin' with Batman in the Batmobile and Batman is married to whatever-the-fuck-her-name-is, that's no good! A henpecked Batman telling a trouble-getting-laid Robin how he *used* to score fuckin' sucks.

Mike was telling me about this woman who wanted him blah-blah-blah, but I had to admit that, for some unknown reason, he did have pretty good luck with women and, as I explained, had landed a gig living rent-free with a women who he complained about a lot so he played up this prowess all the time.

I never could quite figure it. He wasn't leagues beyond me in looks and I knew it couldn't be his job that warranted all the action he claimed he got. My job as a chef had far more cachet than his as one of the three mechanics at 30-Minute Clutch Bunny (twelve locations throughout the area. "We're hoppin' fast"). Granted, Mike *had* worked his way up from the guy in the bunny suit waving at drivers trying to get them to pull in for all-of-a-sudden clutch work to his position as . . . grease monkey, and monkeys *are* farther up the evolutionary ladder than bunnies, but still. Whatever.

We're on our way to visit Randall 'cause Mike has just got to see for sure whether it can all be true. He simply won't believe me. On the seat a big pink rabbit's head sits atop a folded pink rabbit suit.

"What's with the rabbit again?" I ask.

"That fucker Jimmy didn't show up for work again. They made me put on the rabbit costume 'cause I got least mechanic seniority."

"That sucks."

"Hmmmh! You ever wear a rabbit costume for four hours? It's fucking hot in there . . . even in the fuckin' rain! I got totally soaked. Fuckin' ears droopin' and shit . . ."

"Damn." I could suddenly use the word "cherish" in the same sentence with my job.

"The whole costume starts gettin' that wet wool funk. I don't wanna talk about it."

"Well, wait 'til you see Randall," I tell Mike, getting his mind off. "He's gonna want you to call him the D-O-Double G."

"No fucking way."

"Or the Dogg."

"Fuck that!"

"Yeah, just wait."

"Where's he get that shit?"

"He thinks he's Snoop, man. Wait 'til you take a pee, he's got this big ass poster of Ice Cube in the bathroom lookin' all pissed off and shit. It's hard to take a leak sometimes. . . ."

"I hate rap."

". . . Ice Cube starin' you down, you got your dick in your hand . . ."

"Rap sucks."

"Some of it's kinda cool. Actually he's got some pretty good shit."

But we both agree that we can't picture Randall as the D-O-Double G just yet.

"He's lost his fuckin' mind," Mike says.

"At least he gave up on the dreads," I say.

Mike rolls his eyes.

Randall gave up on the dreads when his hair started falling out. He'd lose single dreads the size of a foot-long hot dog one dread at a time. On the top of his head a fat dread would hang on by a few hairs for ten days or so like a loose tooth. Accidentally sitting on a lost dread on his couch could freak the shit out of you.

"Did I tell you what he said last time I saw him?" I ask Mike.

"What the fuck did he say last time?" Mike asks.

"We got some burritos from the Zamorana truck down on East Fourteenth? We're sitting in the car and I got the little containers of hot sauce and I ask him if he wants some?"

I pause because I know if I pause long enough Mike will look at me pissed off and yell, "What the fuck did he say?!" and when he does I tell him,

"He says, and I swear, 'I'm not that loc-ed-out nigger that you thought I was.' "

"What?!"

"Yeah, over hot sauce. And he's serious! He drives all the way down to that Muslim bakery in Oakland. What is *that* about?"

"He's fucked up."

"His girlfriend's kinda cute."

"And she's *black*?" Mike asks like it's too much.

"Yeah. I went out with this black chick once."

"Whatever."

As the talk is now steered sufficiently close to women I tell him about the Jane fiasco (in that had-to-let-her-go light that I'm most comfortable with).

"Fuck her," Mike says and then his face lights up. "Oh! I got somebody for you."

It seems there's a friend of a friend, Marla, and Mike's glad to lend the helping hand, but when he tells me she works for some big computer firm, I balk. It's usually a dead-giveaway bad sign because I'm just never the BMW-drivin' SWM that those kind of SWFs are usually in the market for and I'd already had a bad experience with one of them. Once I hear she works in Mountain View that's it, but Mike (who in reality doesn't even know this woman; Marla has asked for available men for her friend) assures me that she's just my type.

"But you don't even know her, do you?" I protest to Mike.

"Well, technically."

"Technically?"

He nods in a weirdly encouraging manner.

"Have you ever even met her?" I ask.

"Marla told me I met her at a Christmas party last year."

"Did you?"

"I think so; I don't really remember exactly."

"What does she look like?"

He's shaking his head like he can't really remember at all. "She's got some great job. . . ."

"What does she look like?"

"And! And, she actually reads. You've been wanting to meet someone who actually reads, right?"

I think about Anastasia. "I don't know. . . . What does she look like?"

"Marla says she's good-looking. What have you got to lose? A few hours?"

"Why don't *you* meet her then?"

"I'm livin' with Kat, remember? Besides, I don't do blind dates anymore. I'm beyond threshold. I've gone on too many bad blind dates."

"See?! They're just no good."

"Yeah, but you're not at threshold. There's still hope for you. You could become like our shining example."

"What the fuck are you talking about?"

"You could be like the Neil Armstrong of blind dates. 'PSSSHHH!! One small step for man . . . PSSSHHH!' History is riding on this."

"She's a total skank, right?"

"Skank?! Oh, man! Where do you get this? You've only been on, what, three, four bad blind dates?"

"Does the Internet count?"

"I guess, but what I'm getting at is there's still hope. PSSHHH!! One giant leap for—"

"Would you stop with the 'PSSHHH!!' already?! It's really not convincing me."

"Just do this one favor, huh?"

"You're begging."

"Come on, dude."

"You know I hate it when you beg." The light bulb at last goes off over my head. "Oh, I get it. You're after Marla."

"Me?! I got a woman." He says it in such a way that I instantly know he is. A little side action with Marla. The part I didn't get was that we both know Marla. The boys all know about Marla. Marla is trouble from the get-go. An emotional speed trap, a dive bar filled with bad-brained bikers. She has Pain and Trouble written all over the place like "redrum." I once had three different men in my living room all of whom had slept with her, every one of them in angry agreement (a minimum of six months after the fact and none of them laughed off their involvement—"Oh, yeh, heh-heh, that Marla"—No, this was an angry bonding over the fact that each one of them had been pushed to the point of screaming into the phone either to Marla directly or to her answering machine, "Fucking stop calling me! It's over. Stop harping on it!").

It's not like Marla was begging them back. No, Marla was one of those people who can't quite figure out when it's over. The debriefing often outlasted the initial involvement. Marla liked to call the boys and yell about how fucked they were.

So why do they continue to fall? Why would my friend be after Marla rather than the Blind Date? Because first off she was a known quantity, a bad quantity, but known nonetheless and, therefore, preferable to the possible excruciating one to two hours known as the Blind Date.

And Marla's second winning characteristic was that she was one of those fall-in-your-lap kind of girls. The kind where the path to the bedroom didn't take on the dimensions of a major Caltrans post—major earthquake project (full-scale chain-gang road crews manning the lines, making the many dates, the promptly returned phone calls, dinners, tickets, flowers and the slow moving around the bases to home plate).

With Marla you didn't have to try and score like you were playing for the 1980s St. Louis Cardinals—a bunt single, a stolen base, a fielder's choice advancing the runner and, finally, the sacrifice fly. With Marla it was strictly McGuire: a series of strikeouts (she took no offense; she was often drunk and didn't mind the attention) followed by the sudden dramatic home run. Boom! You're scored.

That's what Mike was after. He was angling on a certain light at that certain time in some certain bar after a certain number of drinks and you're both getting that certain sort of feeling and Bam! His juice card. He'd remind her of the favor he'd done, getting her sad and lonely friend a date with a complete stranger.

After mostly getting rid of the notion of calling Marla up myself, I reluctantly agree and Mike puts in his single request.

"Don't actually meet her until after this weekend. Okay?" He has that grin on his face meaning he was begging again and technically he's also at the very least allowing for the fact that I might bungle the blind date so badly that Marla would have a bone to pick with him when that certain moment came around rather than the other way around.

We pull up to the house. Randall "The D-O-Double G Dogg" Holmes lived in a house that sat more or less directly under an I-80 overpass up by Richmond. It was like Woody Allen's place in *Radio Days* where they live under the roller coaster. Every once in a while you'd have to stop talking while a convoy of semis rumbled past, the walls practically vibrating with the noise.

"W'sup," Randall greets us with a gangstery nod and scowl.

"Oh." Mike is already disgusted by the sight of the cute piggish little pit bull puppies scrambling at Randall's—excuse me, Tha Dogg's feet.

"Chill," I tell Mike.

Randall begins to bob his head rhythmically and asks, "Let's go on into tha crib."

"Cool," I say and we follow him into his house.

We sit down in his living room. A *Jet* magazine sits on the table, a big poster about how we can all trace our heritage to Africa is on the wall. I remember back when Randall was this white kid from the flats of West Berkeley. English-Irish, I believe.

"You boys wan sum forties?" Randall asks.

"Sure," I say.

"A forty? What the fuck is that?!" Mike opens with his usual gambit of light hostility. "How 'bout a beer? You got a 'beer,' Rand?"

"It's Tha Dogg." Randall hikes up his enormous Ben Davis coveralls, fakes some signs and says, "You wanna hang in my crib, it's Tha Dogg!"

Mike stares at him for a moment. "All right, Dogg."

While the D-O-Double G's is in the kitchen getting beer Mike tells me not all that quietly, "I don't think I'm gonna be able to deal with this shit."

"Chill. He's got some serious chronic, G," I try to explain to Mike.

"I ain't callin' him Tha Dogg all night."

"You better recognize," Randall's voice comes loudly from the kitchen.

fresh meat

Dave, our very own black-market-kind-bud-, wild-'shroom and abs procuring hippie freewheeling philosophizing purveyor, drove this beat-up old car that was coated from head to toe with a variety of dried pasta shapes. Every square inch of Dave's '69 VW Bug was covered with the raw sienna of fine faded dried semolina. It's how they first met, Marco being something of an amateur scholar on pastas, their shapes and origins.

Most all of the foods Marco loved came with a tale involving romance, dumb luck or a war-or-crop-failure-induced ingredient shortage. In the greatest dishes either someone was trying to win someone's heart or the thing got fucked up and somehow came out better than ever. Marco even claimed a small skirmish flared into a minor European war involving some island, the Duke of Mahon and a bloody battle over—if I understood him correctly—the recipe to the newly discovered Mayonaisse.

"The Duke of Mahon—?" Marco insisted. "Well . . . ?"

"Yeah," I was forced to agree, "and why is it Hellmann's in one half of the country and Best Foods in the other?"

Today Dave delivered to us two fresh abalone from the North Coast. It was technically illegal. You could catch them but not sell them commercially. Marco didn't mind as long as Dave never brought in an undersized one. A bucket would appear by the back door, usually on Sunday, and this Sunday there was a bucket of two black-market North Coast abalone still alive and throbbing in the water. It was the same day the new third waitress started.

We'd lost the latest third waitress the week before. This time it was carpal tunnel syndrome. Moira claimed it was from having to carry too many heavy plates from the kitchen to the dining room.

"That's what a waitress does!" Gina protested when Moira first broke the news. "They carry plates."

Moira was angling for a gig as the Hostess. The hostess is kind of like Diana Ross of the Supremes, part of the same group, but in the lead and possibly wearing a different outfit.

Gina was having none of it, not to mention Marco.

"*I'm* the host," Marco told everyone and no one in particular. "We don't need a hostess. *I'm* the host. It's called Marco's."

Moira just shrugged. She was sporting heavy-duty wrist support devices like she'd just returned from tryouts for the archery or bowling team.

No one would budge so Moira had to leave. As soon as the door closed behind her Gina looked at Marco. "I hope that girl's not thinking she's getting unemployment or disableness."

"Disability," Marco corrected.

"Mmmm." Gina looked disgusted and headed back into the kitchen as Marco rummaged through the drawer looking for waitress resumes.

I prepped up the abs. Cut and pried them out of their shells, cleaned all the guts and black meat around the perimeter until there was just the cephalopod of fresh abalone like some fat squat flesh-colored erasure of meat. Then I sliced them thin as paper. They'd peel away from the slicer like semistiff tree trunk sections. I would batter them in flour and egg and sauté them in butter a minute a side, just enough to brown the batter. I decided to serve them with some potato gnocchi left over from Saturday night, toss it in fresh basil butter, with maybe some rabe or spinach or chard on the side.

I ate a couple slices right off the bat. Check the seasoning in the flour, you know. The distinct texture and perfumey seafood flavor melted in my mouth and put a smile on my face.

I was happy as a clam. Tonight the new girl was working. Word raced through the kitchen like lightning fire. Whoever was first would walk back shaking his head or his hand like it got burnt: "You should see this new waitress they just hired."

The new girl. She'd never be hotter than those first few weeks. Amber. I even had a hand in hiring this one. Maybe it was destiny. I hadn't had a waitress for a while. Maybe something good might come my way, November's rains be damned.

We didn't get many babes working at Marco's despite our re-volving third waitress policy because Gina was none too keen on hiring any young thang that Marco was too obviously drooling over and she knew his type on top of it (he fell for the blondies, blue eyes, bangs, tall and thin; that was his ticket. He didn't care about a rack on 'em. "A pretty face," he'd tell me, "you young men can't even appreciate a beautiful face, but someday . . . ," and he'd nod knowingly).

But Gina had been sick the past week and Marco'd worked a bunch of doubles covering Moira's shifts and I'd covered a few in the kitchen as well and I guess we rewarded ourselves. Being the conscientious employee that I was (not to mention Supreme Over-lord of All Things Kitchen during Gina's absence) one night as we sat at the Table I reminded Marco of the blonde that had walked in after lunch a couple of weeks earlier looking for work. She was just his type and though not mine I sensed in her a disaster magnet that while not necessarily attractive often spelled availability.

His eyes lit up and he looked in the drawer where they kept the resumes. "Carlo! You're a good man. I'll blame you when the time comes."

Now Marco just wanted to flirt, as was his nature. He couldn't help himself really. It was all innocent, just the hint of hope, the threat of more to keep his blood going. But to Gina it was a breach of their love, unforgivable in any form and often on Sunday nights when it was Maxie, Marco, Rock'n'Rollero, the third waitress and me, he'd come into the kitchen and tell me how hard it was for him to be a responsible committed faithful man while still retaining his manness.

"Gina would kill me." He was sipping a fine tobacco-ey Nebbiolo d'Alba. "She doesn't understand how a man works. Italian women, they just don't. They always want to fight to the bloody end and try and change your nature. And I've seen many a man finally give up . . . Mmmm. And you think *they're* faithful?!"

"Women?" I asked.

"Gina! . . . Well, yes, women," Marco reconsidered. "What I mean is *Italian* women. Hah! But you! You don't have to worry about that. You're single."

He said it as though it were gold. I lived in a world he idealized after his ten years with Gina. Single. It rang of freedom to Marco. No more nobody telling you nothing. You could do as you please when and where you please. You could look at the women in a different light. They were suddenly available now that you were available. But I knew how that worked. It didn't turn out to be such an easy thing.

But Marco didn't want to hear about the minutiae of the process—the wheels set in motion, the foundations laid, the fruitless thirty-day siege of Miss Stalingrad, the Crazy Janes dumped in your lap. He just wanted to hear about the girls. What was her name? What was she like? What color were her eyes, her hair? Tell me of the quality of her smile.

Marco loved to hear any stories I had involving girls: the kisses, the second-base activities, the rare hot and ready ones. We both lamented the fact that I didn't have more material, but at least Marco was happy as to my single status.

I just couldn't figure it. I'd have traded places with him in a minute. In a sense. Despite my allegiance to Free and Single I could see that Gina was a good woman and you could see they got along and the rarity of that was slowly, reluctantly dawning on me. And you'd think that'd be enough. You'd think *something* could be enough.

blind date

And so I'm off on a date despite the bad weather. Is it Amber? you ask. No. Apparently she finds me completely uninteresting and I nearly sense an attraction toward Rock'n'Rollero on her part. No, I'm on my way to meet Mike's blind date woman, a woman who I'm sure will slump very slightly, but still perceptively (my eyes note movement very well) upon seeing me.

I want to approach this thing with a certain devil-may-care je ne sais quoi, but how can I? The matrix of the loser nature of the situation (I still can't believe how word leaked out at work; I mentioned something to Gina and now Rock'n'Rollero knows) combined with the weather plays heavily on my mind.

It can play very clearly whenever the sky turns gray and the pavement turns wet and the gutters fill with rushing water. The near-dank smell of freshly fallen rain kills me sometimes.

. . . She and I met on such a day. It was a downpour in June, well beyond the usual time for a downpour, and one month later, our first night together, a rain slipped in unforeseen and unexpected, leaving the morning fresh, the ground moist and an entire world born (I want to exchange these memories, trade them in for something new, but what can one do? There is no brain/memory liposuction invented yet).

And tonight it rains as I head over the bridge into San Francisco and I measure up this poor woman I'm going to meet against these visions of love conceived in the fresh-fallen rain. What am I thinking?! For now rain can be bleak and sad to me and the coming winter frightens me sometimes.

"You kissed me," she said with true surprise and happiness. It was her first time over at my place, where I live to this day. I'd cooked her dinner, we'd seen a show and now she was at my place. I could see she was going for the chair and I'd never reach her then and perhaps I was more bold or the moment more right back then or I was emboldened by the utter dark unknowing beauty of her face (she didn't realize the jewel she held; I want to snatch it from her now). I stepped up to her, gently took her hand and slowly leaned in . . .

"You kissed me," she said, and that smile, the wonderful amazing acceptance is burned into my fucking mind tonight as I go to meet someone who I know will suck or hate me.

AIYEEEH!! AIYEEEH!!

AIYEEEH!! AIYEEEH!!

The Monster . . . She screams at me as I head over the bridge, into the City, to a neighborhood very near to where . . . She now lives.

So I was up in her room. The Blind Date Girl!? Yes! She was actually quite attractive, kind of my type (which made me imagine she found me troll-like, but she'd accepted a second date so onward I plodded). I could hardly believe it. The entire atmosphere was amped up. It was a neat apartment, but not too neat. Too neat is always a bad sign or too stark as though they're operating out of the address rather than living there. No, this one was good. Nice wood floors, blond.

"I wish my floors looked like these," I said, smiling.

"Hmm? Oh, they're okay. You want something to drink?"

"Sure." I continued my tour. There was a big bookcase filled with interesting books: Kerouac, *I Ching*, Chaucer, Faulkner. There wasn't an Austen in sight. Hope still breathed.

She was in the kitchen readying some sort of a beverage because without the beverage pretty much nothing at all can take place between the sexes. She was getting me a beer, an Anchor Steam; she had one of her own already open. Good, good, good, I'm thinking, and begin to try and quietly take up the reins of this evening.

Her music collection was a little too sensitive for me because I've never been able to lose the angry loud music that many fifteen-year-olds are initiated into. Luckily, our tastes overlapped nicely in the presixties department. I put on some Basie.

We settled onto the couch, a little ways apart, but not too far, talking about our families, where we came from, where we grew up, what brought us here, for it seems most of us here are immigrants of some sort. It was nice. She was quick and smart and had this mischievous smile.

And she did two things during the evening that stuck in my head. Not quite gulp, lump-in-the-throat department, but they held potential future significance. I had made a comment about her books, about how impressed I was at her tastes, and she started reciting something which caught me a bit off guard because I secretly fear the woman with hidden actress dreams who suddenly bursts into character and now you have to play the audience (and love the performance). But as I listened it became beautiful—the words she spoke—and then I slowly began to recognize it. It was Kerouac. From *On the Road*.

And then as if that wasn't enough, later on there was almost a "moment." We were sitting at a table toward the back of the club, listening to but unable to see the band playing (it was a swing band dressed in vintage clothes and people dressed in vintage

clothes were doing the lindy hop, again confirming to me the ut-
terly shattered nature of Time. It had lost all sense of itself and lay
pell-mell Pollock-splattered), talking about movies. I brought up
Notorious as almost a test, one of my covert early dating measuring
and gauging devices. I'll always love Hitchcock's *Notorious*. *Notorious*
represented to me the most poignant form of Love, the excruciating
Unrequited Love totally idealized and teetering on the brink of
happening. The Love that might be missed because of circumstance.

It was a movie that would never fail to have me weeping waves
of tears over Love I didn't have. I encapsulated all my sorrow of
love longing in *Notorious*. One scene in particular. The park bench.

"Oh, and the scene on the park bench." I could hardly believe
it when she brought it up. She was right there with me and faked
collapsing from the tension and touched my forearm briefly. Our
eyes met through the incredible haze of secondhand smoke and time
froze in silence for a flash. I looked away nervously.

She mentioned the bench scene! I can't believe it! I felt my cold
girded heart begin to melt for a moment. Damn!

The rest of the evening had a pleasurably nervous air to it and
when I dropped her off, as she got out of the car she leaned in and
gave me a little kiss on the cheek. She had that mischievous little
smile again. One that seemed to have just escaped and was looking
for fun knowing full well Master was not far behind with the leash.

Her eyes glowed for a flash, little shiny black marbles, and her
mouth was filled with tiny sharp teeth that were only the slightest
bit crooked with two gaps, one front top center, and you know
what they say that means, but right then I was off the scent for
the saddle and as I drove home over the beautiful Bay Bridge I felt
electrified and pondered, instead, the implications of her shiny eyes
and Cary Grant, Ingrid Bergman and Jack Kerouac on a park bench
through a mellow haze of two martinis.

gina

'Twas the risotto brought me back. The next time I came completely to I had a wooden spoon in my hand and was stirring away
on a pot of polenta, some eggplant slices broiling away on the grill.
I had my eye on them. Gina was to my left. She was cooking a big
pot of risotto. That's what I was mainly watching.

It was around five o'clock and for once we were actually set up,
just some finishing touches, simply waiting (hoping was more like
it) for the dinner rush to begin. No one said a word; it was only
the sounds of the kitchen and whatever my mind might throw up
for consideration.

Gina and I were side by side, me stirring the pot of the night's
polenta, she stirring up the pot of the night's risotto. I was a bit
jealous. The risotto's more fun; there's more art to it. But Gina
said,

"Polenta! You all think polenta is so easy to make—boil it for
ten minutes with a few stirs. Hah!" She wagged a wooden spoon
at me like a conductor's baton. "No, polenta is like a good woman,
she takes a little while to soften up."

Of course, I said to myself. Women take a while. I vowed to put
that information to good use for once.

Gina nearly smiled at me and right then I kind of thought she
was quite beautiful. The times working shoulder to shoulder like
this evening I might slip into a fantasy of her. I'd watch her work
out of the corner of my eye when we would be silently setting up
for the night's service. Rock'n'Rollero off to the side some nights,
inconsequential in his rock and roll world. Gina was so absorbed
and so careful about every detail. The lines in her face (lines that
had their roots in frowns and anger) would soften then in the com-
pletion of the task, and that's when my fantasy of her would grow.

The thing you'd notice as she prepared some great dish was the
fierce excitement in her eyes. They had a clear dark beauty about
them. That and her hair; her hair was so very straight, so very black
and cut to a very uniform length midway down her neck. I mention
her hair not just because of the way the jet blackness, the glowing
blue blackness of it, accented her thin arched black eyebrows and
olive skin, but because her personality always seemed to me the
exact opposite of her hair. She should have had longer, more flow-
ing, thick, wavy, rich and wild hair. Her black hair in its perfect
straight and neat trim of length was the only thing ever predictable
about Gina.

The dusk was deepening and the kitchen began to grow in the
hums and murmurs that made up itself: the smell of the simmering
stock, the clanking of plates slid into the dishwasher, the tapping
of knives against cutting boards, spoons clacking against pots.

The pot of just-simmering chicken stock combined with that
dreamy thick smell of simmering Arborio Gina worked at caught
my attention. We were both stirring and had a silent rhythm between us. It was crystal clear and true, when the Realness Quotient
had reached saturation. One hundred percent. Not a word.

I was the force stirring the wooden spoon in the pot of cornmeal;
the weight of the mush against the spoon, the dull clacks it would

make against the inside of the pot were my all. Gina was the force behind the wooden spoon stirring the petulant rice; it would spit and suck when she scraped the bottom up. I could feel the buzzing of the moment. Risotto and polenta.

pride and passion

After work I decided to become, in a way, more like Cary Grant in my dealing with women. "In a way," I say, because ultimately I didn't take too well to the oily charm of Cary Grant.

He was just 🌹 much too gay for me. He lacked Newman's Greek God face undeniableness and Gary Cooper's tall guy in Hollywood with a donkey dick swagger, but there was something about Grant. He almost couldn't be troubled (same as Mitchum but with Mitchum you also think he's not often all that interested and just wondering where the next shot and bong load are coming from), but Cary was instantly ready, a cat springing into action from statue form. That was the thing about Cary Grant. And it killed me that I met a woman who quoted Kerouac and knew the park bench scene with Bergman. The movie was going to be on cable when she came over next. It was like some rare meteor shower alignment of the cosmos. Romance is wired that evening.

I decided there was only one thing to do. One last bit of research into Love and Romance and my icon of both dreams sat there on the mantle of the fireplace that doesn't fire. Sophia Loren. It's a black-and-white still of her in the soaked dress in *Boy on a Dolphin*.

I headed out to Movie Image, to the Wizard, to find out if there was a movie starring both Cary Grant and Sophia Loren. He knew instantly. Every single bit of his movie knowledge which seemed to be comprised of every single bit of movie fact seemed to be always at the tip of his brain. At all times.

"Oh, well, *Houseboat*, yes, and there's *Pride and the Passion*; Sinatra's in that, too. It's not out on video yet." He looked up at me, nodding, and headed toward the stacks. "*Houseboat*. It's rented." He held the box up toward me and managed his half-smile for the .65 seconds that was his max. "It's a comedy."

"A comedy?!" That ruined my whole theory practically. A comedy won't do. "Damn!" I knew there was no point but I asked him for the thousandth time, "*Boy on a Dolphin?*"

The Wizard shook his head sadly. "Not out on video. I'll call you as soon as we can track one down."

I went for my backup babe in *The Killers*.

I decided to go next door. I was a brave man that night and hoped to challenge one of my demons. Cut it down in one fell swoop, one bloody battle. Have done with it once and for all. That remained the idea despite all past data.

Sun Hong Kong is where I headed.

The potstickers.

I pushed the door open with the bravado of a Clint Eastwood and surveyed the situation: my need for potstickers and my lookout for that one waiter.

The potstickers and that same Chinese waiter.

There he was.

He was there every goddamned night no matter what. The only explanation is that he worked 365 nights a year, but my American Capitalist/Consumer forty-hour workweek mind cannot conceive of such a thing. The only other possibility was magic or some cryptic sign from the cosmos (it's not bad enough that the cosmos rarely leaves signs, but when they or he or she does, it comes in riddles and via foggy apparitions).

Either way, there he was. The sun was down and there he was and I ordered my potstickers. To go. Clutching my lonely guy home alone video movie for the night, my caste was marked for all who sat in the bustling dining room eating BBQ pork fried rice, roasted duck thighs ly fun soup—big fucking steaming bowls of it—spicy saday beef chow fun and whole gingered crab taken fresh from the tanks against the far walls. There were lots of Asian diners which gave me confidence in the food and so what if it is to go? So fucking what?! I've got Ava Gardner, who's hot as shit even if she can't hardly act and's in mostly cheesy movies.

I pay some more of my money and head out the door with my second little package. The rain has just begun to fall. It's only a slight mist but I can feel it (and I'd seen the forecasts of Mr. TV Weatherman from the night before), a big storm be a-brewin', and I head home in an excitement of the weather to come, to the dry comfort of my home—can't wait. I'm gonna love those potstickers and crank up the heat and with the movie I can tell it's gonna be enough tonight as I curl up and dream about . . . Aida instead of Ava.

But there *was* a moment. As I sat on one of the three chairs they have right by the cold door, holding the marks of my caste for all to see, some Asian college boys came in and took a quick look and rejected me antlike in my insect inconsequentiality in a way only college boys have mastered and I looked down at the sick linoleum and then looked up at the neon and the pictures that now revealed their full cheese to me in the ugliest of lights and that's when it got caught up there in my throat. Right then I had to take the shallowest of nonbreaths and was forced to remember when it was *us*. When . . . She was here with me. It was *our* place and the pot-stickers were *our* dish. She'd never had them before with the red chili oil and the vinegar, but it didn't matter in the end if she'd ever had them before or not. And whether or not she still used hot chili oil and vinegar. She was gone and it didn't matter anymore, I kept telling myself.

Besides, in her place there's a new girl to hope for. Aida. With her it already seems different. Different than with Nurse! (who I knew from the start) and different than with Jane (who I knew from the start) and different than with Anastasia (with my forced moments of imagined love) and different than with Maria (though I felt the same way toward her at one point).

I was at that perfectly dangerous point of a "relationship." That point before anything has really happened. When only hope has been raised (is it the white flag of surrender or battle flags?). When I knew it was a long shot, when it got scary for a moment, when I couldn't help but dream days and miles away.

Aida. Her name alone was enough to convince me. And her frightened little smile and her tiny tiny fingers and her sparkling black eyes. I grabbed my white plastic bag of potstickers, headed home and couldn't really concentrate on anything, not even the movie and the beautiful Ava. I ignored my vow to avoid love at all costs and spent the night alone, eating Chinese food, dreaming of a girl. Dreaming of Aida.

aida

She greeted me from the top of the stairs, just outside her apartment door. She had on faded Levi's more worn than the last time, venetian blind holes on both thighs. She was a bit old to be called cute, but she looked cute nonetheless with her sort of sheepish/shy smile exposing those tiny teeth I was beginning to notice and lighting up her moist black eyes. Inside her place, when she turned to go to the kitchen for that needed beverage—it was a Sablet—I caught a sight of her backside. She'd made the mistake (or was it all part of her invisible woven web?) of tucking in her shirt, revealing a fine ass. One that came alive in a pair of tight, faded 501s. Often the basis of a meaningful and long-lasting relationship, I've found.

But it was her hands that really amazed me. It was after another fine meal I'd prepared in her house, a risotto. I told her she'd never had a true homemade risotto. That it was one of those dishes, cooked over time and served all at once upon the moment of readiness; that risotto was like love, a dish best not served warmed over (I didn't actually tell her this part).

We were sitting on the couch and I held her hand lightly in my own. Her short fingers were very small around, topped with the tiniest fingernails. Like the hand of a small girl in an adult world.

It must have seemed so harsh to her, I thought—she'd told me the week before the story of a brutal rape when she was younger. She'd look up at the door whenever she heard a sound out in the hallway and was never comfortable with a person behind her. We often had to stand aside to let people pass on the sidewalk.

I wanted to fall in love with her. Right then and there. I wanted the course of the postdinner evening to pass like a 112-minute classic romance. Finally that third-reel kiss, the audience is busting from the tension and so am I right now, here on the couch. The rain pounds outside, it's making the possibility of warm embrace the winter long all the more enticing.

My intentions were even somewhat true. I've dropped for a moment my scoundrel dreams. We're watching *Notorious* on TV and having a great time. So give me your warm self, my brain calls out, but I can see the trouble on her brow as she submits to a short kiss. And in the fading smile that's being dragged back home I can see that she's frightened. She's not quite ready. It's not quite right and I know what she means, but I can't quite help myself. The thing she doesn't get is that sometimes lust and the specter of scary romance is better than waiting out these wet dark days all alone under the sheets. Hot passion's the cure for cabin fever sometimes, don't you know?

going-away party

And then Mike leaves. Bang, just like that. It took about ten days and then Mike was gone. He'd finally at long last anguishing fretfully in some way I could only guess at left Kat by leaving the United States. After a few calls and intermittent just-occurred-to-me ideas, he'd cajoled his way into an ESL teaching position in the pilsnered and tall-lassed green rolling hills of the Czech Republic. It's almost impossible for us not to add Slovakia, but they're two things now. An extra team for the Olympics!

Mike's strong point in the race to be an ESL teacher proved to be the time difference. Every once in a while when he was enthusiastically drunk and merrily buzzed around 2:30 A.M. PDT he'd place a phone call to the Czech Republic, which was just getting ready for the lunch break on the next day. It worked like a charm. After a few tries over eleven months' time? He was off. After bloodsweating over his girl and the little home and life he'd been fretting over all summer? He was gone!

I knew he was serious when he wheeled his BMW motorcycle that never ran over to my flat and we somehow pried open the soggy warped garage door above the abandoned highway concrete strip that was my driveway, buckled by years of apple tree root growth.

He had come up with the obvious plan of calling his woman when he switched planes at Dulles to inform her of the current status of their relationship. He figured that was the best thing. Just tell her over the phone. His fears were twofold. First, the long-distance screaming and weeping he'd be subjected to ("But I ain't putting in any extra change. She's got three minutes to weep and scream," he told me) and, second, the more frightening prospect that she would either torch all the belongings he'd left at the house or at the very least smash some stuff and leave the rest in a pile outside to rot away slowly over the course of the winter. That's why he wheeled the motorcycle over to my place, along with a box containing his shot glass collection and a rare "Jane's Addiction" poster.

He had the ticket in his hand and asked if I'd drive him to the airport. We just had to swoop by the place and get his bags; she should still be shopping at Safeway.

How could I say no? He was like a fugitive. End a relationship with a getaway. Of course?! I promised to try it myself if the situation ever came up.

On our slow drunken drive down to the airport (don't try this at home, kids) we stopped off at every dive bar on San Pablo from Richmond proper to south of Doug's BBQ where we loaded up 'cause we both well knew that while there were reluctant women the world round, the same couldn't be said of good BBQ. So there we were digging hard into our white paper plates, our fingers coated, our faces glistening and the hot sauce working its magic on our brains.

We started talkin' about food, about Q, and we agreed that while Nate's and Doug's was mighty fine BBQ, nothing could match now gone Carmen's. It had survived the mystery murder, but then, six months later, the doors were closed up and word was that the old man just couldn't make a go of it. Niko told me it was a curse, that you just can't get away with some things and murdering a man in the dining room was one of those things.

"What?! You hadn't heard?" Niko's eyes would widen. "Oh yeah, it was the old man did it." Not sweet Carmen, with her hair toweled up in those bright kerchiefs takin' your order with a grand smile, warning you about the incendiary heat of the hot BBQ.

What's in it? I always asked, lookin' for a new recipe, but Carmen would never tell you. Is it scotch bonnet? I asked. Oh, there's chiles in it, all sorts of stuff in it, and then she'd laugh and walk off.

No, it was the old man did it. Happened after hours. After all that thick sweet corn bread was wrapped up and put away, after the simmering stockpots of Jamaican goat curry and the Q-sauce were wrapped up and in the walk-in. There was something fishy about the whole deal. The old man knew the guy so they charged him with murder or manslaughter, but who knows? Maybe it was self-defense against thieves after the curry profits or the Q recipe, but there was a dead guy, somewhere by the counter Niko says, right where you sit down and eat your fuckin' BBQ chicken with that fiery dark red sauce and suck down a Red Stripe; it's Jamaican barbecue, mon!

And then one day the old guy's back, sitting there as usual at the counter in his white T-shirt, watching fucking *Entertainment Tonight!* (na-na-na-na-na-naaa), except his hair is totally fucking white. Every hair. Like he's seen shit no one wants to even imagine, but here comes Carmen: What'll it be, boys? The hot? That's hot, you know. We know, Carmen, make it hot as shit 'cause my boy's going to a land where there are no black folk and there is no sweet corn bread and they do not know the manna that is Q.

This land and wonderful world was all replaced by the plastic buzz-kill overpriced bar at SFO. It sits next to the overpriced Burger King and some overpriced cookie store selling bogus "San Francisco" cookies, like San Francisco has its very own special fucking cookie. You can hear planes roaring in takeoff in the background.

We were drinking on his money now. Mike had a $20 that had fallen into his hands in such a way that he could gladly blow it on us at that last chance saloon.

"But you're gonna get those drinks on the international flight," I said.

"Oh, yeah I am . . . and then some." Mike nodded knowingly, as though he had some sort of international tiny airline flight bottle heist planned by the time the bonny green hills of Ireland showed first land beyond the long Atlantic, and then he suggested one last round if I had three dollars on me. I did.

I headed home. First it was . . . Her. And now Mike. I could feel the heat of existence on my collar.

dave

This is where work came in. Work was the only real and true reference point. Work was my schedule, my clock, my whipping boy, my salvation. Work was out the door and out of mind. Work was money and work marked exactly when it was that I wasn't at work thereby rendering those nonworking times all the more sweet.

It was a wet and soggy afternoon. Winter, which had seemed a welcome change the first couple of storms, was already getting old. I escaped from yet another short downpour by ducking into the warmth of work.

There was always food and if nothing else going to work meant getting a sandwich. And so it was as the rain began to pick up, pounding down upon the pavement. I saw Dave's car parked out front as I walked up. The famous Pastamobile.

By now the storms were almost comical in their ferocity and with the rains pounding at a fairly steady rate, Dave's car had reached al dente stage. The car now left a trail of fallen fusilli and soggy rotelli in its wake. In a light rain it had a strange almost alive look to it, like coral or barnacles on a deepwater wreck.

The kitchen had that immediate warm comfortable feel with the good smell of fine foods and I wondered if I should have a prosciutto Parmesan sandwich for lunch again. I asked myself this almost every

135

day though it was the great unchanging reality of my existence. That I would have a Parma ham and Parmesan cheese on focaccia sandwich in my mitts within ten minutes of donning my apron was the third in my Grand Triumvirate of Imperatives.

The line was quiet. Maxie was at the prep table, his lunch dishes done, peeling some garlic.

"Maxie!" I said.

"Hola, amigo. Como esta?"

"Bien, bien, y tu?"

"Mucho trabajo." Maxie smiled that smile of Maxie's with the glints of gold on the edges of his teeth. He had an Elvis haircut of thick black hair that was combed straight back. Slick and shiny with whatever sort of Mexican hair products guys like Maxie like to use.

Dave had scored big and there were mushrooms to cook. I guess he'd finally gotten enough of his shit together to fire up the bug and head north for some mushroom hunting because on this mushroomy wet day there was Dave in the kitchen, bearing a cardboard box and an excited grin and I could see Rock'n'Rollero was hoping Dave had the bud he'd been waiting on.

"Wait 'til you see this, Carrasco, I got the mother lode," His face was lit up with excitement.

I looked into the box. Dave had scored a large quantity of fresh boletus up in Mendocino.

"Where's the man?" Dave asked.

I nodded toward the dining room.

"Marco!" Dave called and headed to the dining room and I heard a "David" from Marco with his fake Italian accent which he always used when calling out his close friends' names.

The two of them returned to the kitchen and began going over the mushrooms, Marco trying to contain his glee. He picked up an especially large one. Perfect big green brown cap and a fat meaty stem. He couldn't help but smile grandly.

"The toughest part is not running into any of those pot farmers. Those fuckers got guns!" Dave was angling for his price already and I wondered if Marco knew that the bud had been harvested weeks ago.

I pulled out the scale and began to weigh it up.

"I don't know if I can use all these mushrooms." Marco shook his head like it was a damn crying shame.

"Well . . . ," Dave began his soft-sell technique, which was pretty much a simple raising of the eyebrows while implying "I don't know . . ."

We all kinda knew that not too many restaurants were gonna buy from Dave. He leaned a little too far toward the street-persony side of the Green Party's look and not all restaurateurs could appreciate a car covered with dried pasta, imported or not.

It was seven and a half pounds of the "fabuloso grade porcini," as the Italians like to call it. They were selling down at the markets for nearly ten bucks a pound and these were delivered and of exceptional quality.

Marco began filling out the official Dave tab, a three-by-five with a drawing on one side that Marco would make, thus sealing the deal, the tab on the other. This time: one dinner, two sandwiches, a couple of spicy olive and bread apps. He tapped a beer and pulled a twenty out of the drawer. "Well?" Marco's voice always carried with it the air that his first was also his final offer.

Dave took a big swig off the beer, grabbed the twenty and motioned his head toward the dining room. "Now, I've been checking into Heidegger . . ."

"Heidegger?!" Marco scoffed as they headed off to the Table. "He's a German. What could *he* possible know?"

I was left with the porcinis, and they were fine indeed. Moist but not at all soggy; he must have got them before this last rain. My first thought was risotto.

"It's too slow for risotto," Gina told me. "If we did the business like we should? Then risotto."

"How 'bout in a ragout for polenta."

"They only like to order pasta. They think polenta is too simple. No, let's make a little more tagliatelli. There's still some left over from lunch. Dice up the mushrooms and sauté them in olive oil with a little minced shallot and garlic, a splash of white wine and then a small amount of reduced chicken stock, not a lot, I don't, well, you know how I like it."

I was nodding. "With the fresh parsley and Reggiano?"

"Shaved."

"Of course." Gina liked her Parmesan shaved for many of the dishes, felt it left it more up to the diner what to do with it.

And we had the couscous which I was particularly fond of that week. Made in chicken stock with salt and some extra virgin and served with tuna that reflected rainbow light at the right angle, near sashimi grade, grilled rare.

Gina and I stood behind the stoves that night with our tuna and porcinis and tagliatelli wondering where the customers were.

tarte tatin

I'd grown tired of my usual zabaglione (it had gotten me nowhere with Anastasia) and decided to seduce Aida with a Tarte Tatin. It was a dish that came with Marco's blessing. While Gina was the great cook, Marco was the romantic and so it was to him I went for my cooking strategy. He could dream it up, he just couldn't whip it up. I asked him about dessert and he concurred.

"Absolutely. Dessert and the proper choice of wine. We want to get them slightly loosened up with the alcohol, not drunk." He looked at me sternly.

"I know." He took me for such a scoundrel. "I need to get an ice cream machine," I decided. "Some just out of the oven palmiers with handmade vanilla ice cream?"

"Forget the ice cream," Marco told me. "It's winter. The main thing is to keep it small. Have the dessert look small so they don't feel so guilty. And nicely sweet. And forget the coffee. A half-bottle of dessert wine. We're looking for a mood here. And start the evening with a lively, fun wine. Not your brooding too young reds. That's your problem—you choose your women like your red wines. Too young. Irresistible, yes, but they're not ready."

He was losing me. I was glad Rocker'n'Rollero had left. We were sitting at the Table. Amber, the juggling third waitress, still had the smell of fresh meat about her and while I dreamt of Aida I still fantasized having my way with Amber in the dry storage over a twenty-five-pound bag of corn meal set atop a few cases of canned Italian tomatoes. Waitresses (and I can hardly believe I haven't hooked up with one by now and bred at least a maître d' if not a four-star chef) don't all have that smell, that look in their eye, that swing to their walk, that primal pheromone experience, but Amber did. Unfortunately, she spoke to me only slightly more than Rock'n'Rollero did.

I told Marco the story of the Tarte Tatin. The story of a pastry involving the filial duty of two obedient daughters and a fortunate mishap. He was ecstatic.

Somewhere in France there lived a Monsieur Tatin, and Père Tatin loved his apple tart. He loved it so much that he required one each and every day. I don't know if he polished it off himself, if he shared it with friends, if his two daughters were allowed a slice, but every day he required this tart. One day the sisters produced a fine tart incorporating the brainstorm of caramel to accent the soft-baked yielding tart sweetness of the apples. From the smells coming from the oven and the soothing golden blush of the pastry as they pulled it out, the sisters knew they had a winner. That's when disaster struck. At some unfortunate moment (and when you later bake one you realize the mistake had to happen at just the right moment for the tart to turn) the tart was dropped and landed facedown on the kitchen floor! Père Tatin sat waiting in the dining room. Employing an ancient, a tried-and-true kitchen technique, they slipped a serving platter underneath and scooped it up as quickly and neatly as could be, picked off any obvious debris and covered some of the damaged sections with silky white crème fraîche.

Papa was ecstatic! It was the finest tarte he'd ever had. Caramelized apples atop the fine Tatin sisters' pastry? It was such a success that they opened a restaurant and the tarte was all the rave, upside down, apples and caramel. It was served at Maxim's in Paris and the Tatin sisters are immortalized in the pages of *Larousse Gastronomique.*

My dreams were of a more fleshy and humble scope. I've made the caramel in an old iron skillet that has remained truer than any woman in my life. It's so seasoned you can cook eggs in it. Aida is watching; she has the greatest smile, her glass of wine poised in the air. I place the peeled apples in the pan and they sizzle as they hit the hot caramel and then goes the pie crust. This one felt good from the start. It's been resting in my refrigerator since yesterday getting loose and relaxed. It rolled out like butter and I laid its thick cloth likeness over the apples, tucked in the sides. I crossed my fingers. I'd never had all the apples slip from the pan onto the pastry in perfect golden caramel concentric apple circles but I kept waiting for the moment as though it might change my life.

Okay, here's what you do: you make a perfect pie crust and you eighth some apples. How many? Well, enough to perfectly fill the iron skillet. You make a fine brown caramel with sugar and butter in that pan and lay the apple eighths fat sides down in circles and cover it with that pastry and bake it hot, at 400 degrees, 'til it bubbles and browns. Pull it out and at some exact moment it will flip perfect onto a plate. Too soon and it can crack up, too late and the apples will stick.

I banked upon the apples flipping out perfectly, same as tearing the Michelob label and hitting red meant you were going to get some. Perfect tart? Pussy. How could it be any other way? I slipped it into the oven.

MIRROR CHECK

I flip on the light and lock the door to the bathroom. I've just delivered a rather well-received quip and have decided to take a pee and size things up. Let Aida cool her heels in my freshly swept and tidied living room, sort of bask in my limelight.

I examined my reflection: I'm now thirty-six, with credit on life support, my looks fading, my head hinting at later aching. My pocket contains thirteen dollars, my shoes are good and I've got an okay job. I'm quite healthy save for mysterious and vanishing chest pains that come and go late at night and the rapid expansion and contraction of my existence that has been occurring lately, and while the hints of later wreckiness are at last emerging I realize I'm at that crossroads age when a properly dimly lit room can do a lot for me (it's why I bought the rheostat for the living room overhead lamp). While most men might have focused on possible new clothes or hairstyles or better-paying jobs or at least concentrated on the entrees, I'm confident in my strategy of stepping up activity in the desserts department.

The tart's in the oven and I'm sitting there on the couch getting the sneaking suspicion that I've hit yet another reluctant one. A sweetheart who reads books and likes to go to bookstores and likes old movies, who has a sweet smile and dark eyes, who looks good in tight Levi's and is smaller than me. But her kisses are dead.

The first time I tried to write it off as shyness or that it took her a while to warm up to the moment, that it was all too much all too quickly. So the second time around I tried again, after we'd had another pleasant date—eaten our little meal, taken a stroll, prowled the bookstores (we each bought a used copy of James's *Turn of the Screw* to see what all the fuss was about)—and then it was back to my place and I could see she wasn't initiating a damn thing. Such has been my lot as of late and I took that in stride. She *did* sit on the couch, leaving me full of hope—God, was I full of hope—and now this fourth time, our fifth meeting, I lean in again and . . . I don't know, it's not like she tries to stop me, she doesn't say no, but she turns kisses into tiny pecks and then it's back to the conversation or whatever the fuck it was we're doing on the fucking couch when we should be rolling around in each other's arms. When I should be sliding my hands under her fuzzy sweater, when she's supposed to start grabbing me if not for dear life at least like it meant something. It was fucking raining outside, winter was only going to get colder and wetter and here we were in the warm dry living room. Neither one of us were that impressed with the goddamned Henry James short novel for chrissakes! What more do we need to suggest it's time for a little love?

But no. She's another graduate of the Mahatma Gandhi Institute of Make-out Discouragement. It's a passive yet extremely effective method of cooling off the most ardent and hopeful of kissing boys (or at least transferring their sexual lust into frustrated anger). They learn a number of moves at the Institute. There's the last-minute turn-away that transforms a full kiss on the lips into an ineffective peck on the cheek. There's the chin-to-the-chest defensive posturing that leaves no access to the mouth at all. There's the full-body lean-away (with the added stiff arm usually resorted to in later rounds), the use of pillows as a sort of sandbagging protection against your rising waters and then, finally, most sadly of all, the one that finally does it for me, the Dead Kiss.

The Dead Kiss is deadly indeed. It can be full on the lips; there can be tongues involved. Actually, the more intimate the form of the kiss, the more effective the deadness. She lets you kiss her, she doesn't fight you off, there's just nothing there when you arrive. There's no electricity. It's not alive. She hangs from you limp and unaffected. It's as though your kiss has temporarily lobotomized her and then, as if absolutely nothing has happened—and, really, absolutely nothing has; that's the point—she gets up to go to the bathroom.

Now I'm left cooling *my* heels, warm smells coming from the kitchen, thinking I don't quite fit into Aida's Life Plans (regardless of how the tart turns out). Something about me: an element lacking in my conversation, a crudeness in my humor, a psychic scent I give off. Something, for I have yet to receive the password allowing me into her conceived future, a club I'm still rather ambivalent about since I'm supposed to be a swinging bachelor kind of guy, but this ambivalence is drowned out by the screaming desire to quench my thirst.

The irony is that our privates are calling out to each other. I don't care to what she'll testify. It's what's making her frown ever so slightly after she sits back down beside me and asks cheerfully "Is the tart ready yet?"

Despite the wonderful smells of that fine tart coming from the kitchen all is not as it should be. An ancient part of our animal brain prowls about lost in time, thinking as it did in the days when a hairy back was a good thing, when a simple fuck would have been the answer. It would have made animal sense in a satisfying way I find near legendary in my modern paved silicon image-saturated cellular processor. I want to be an animal again and roll about in animal lust with no play-by-play or pregame analysis, and in my excitement I pull her toward me.

"I told you I want to take it slow." She seems serious now. I've gone too far and I must have leaned away a bit too dramatically.

"What?" she asks.

"What do you mean, 'What?' "

She's doing the tiny head shake thing. It means a million No's. "I can't believe you rolled your eyes."

"Huh?"

"I can't ask you to go slow?"

"I didn't roll my eyes," I protest. Did I?

"Yes you did."

I roll my eyes.

"There! You did it again. I want to go slow."

"You can go however you (fucking) want!"

The twelve-second silence is excruciating. My forehead is hotter than the sizzling apples in the oven. I've just about had it. I'm ready to move abroad. Tomorrow. I'll meet up with Mike. I've had it with American women in their thirties.

"I'm gonna check the tart," I say.

"Mmm, you do that." Now she's mad.

I open the oven and pull it out. The tart is perfectly browned, the apple juices bubbling through little holes in the pastry. I'm so pissed off that I don't give a fuck about it. Fuck you, tart, I'm yelling in my hot brain. Fuck the Tatin sisters.

I don't wait a second, I just take the pan and angrily flip it and like a perverse joke that can't help but put a smirk on my face, the tart drops cleanly onto the plate. It came out perfect! Every single apple laid out in a flawless circular pattern. It was beautiful.

We eat the sweet tart but it does not wash away the bitter mood. I sit far away from her and she never makes any move to reconcile and within minutes of finishing dessert she takes her leave with a nervous "I'd better get going."

I'm sitting there hot from the entire evening—the emotions, the wine, the girl. Her uncomfortability makes me love her and hate her all the more. I'm dying to love her and can't help but hate her all at the same time.

"What's the matter?" I ask. "Don't you like me?" I ask this because I know she's nice enough to say she likes me, thus lessening my feeling of rejection.

"I know it sounds stupid . . ."

"What?"

She tsks and screws up her mouth. "It's just . . . It's me. I can't handle it when it gets emotional. It's always the same. If it starts getting intimate . . ." She looks at me in a sad serious way. "I thought I was ready; I guess I'm not."

I realize it's not about me at all (this is both insult and relief). She's flashing back on an entire life's history. I remember her story of the rape horror, followed by that one guy she was with for three years who turned out to be a big fucking asshole, cheating on her.

I've stumbled onto another train wreck. She's as wrecky as me, if not more. There's smoke drifting across a scorched earth and I feel like Chris in *Platoon*.

That's why all the books, I realized. The poetry, the happy and profound world of beauty and sadness she might slip into. Love rose in my head for a moment again like some demon there on the couch and I wondered why she couldn't just as easily slip into *me*, slip into a warm embrace, a hot kiss. My aim is true with this girl, there's the irony, but I'm not nearly as safe as the books and I ended up scaring her away.

She actually left in tears. She said she was sorry for wasting my time and that I was a nice man and, and, well, she was never to be heard from again. She ran off down my stairs into the driving rain and the night.

It was to her books she returned after this date, never to be heard from again, never to return any of my calls. The girl that loved *Notorious* and read books. How can that be?

Could one be ruined for love? Is that possible? That life's love has already come and gone, leaving you somehow jaded or condemned to seek heights of love never again to be realized. I just couldn't imagine it. I could not accept a world where such a notion was possible. That I'd had my chance and the rest was just second-best at best.

Well, fuck it then, I think. Fuck love! I was back on my original mission.

downshift

You know, I'd like to be able to bust out with some great sort of Hollywood plot at some point: bank robbery; gorgeous rich woman (who, unbeknownst to me, is deeply involved with the Japanese Mafia) hires me for lots of money to do her and cook an occasional gourmet meal; the appearance of a genie that evolves into a metaphor of man's struggle for identity; I discover a heretofore unknown talent at playing the ponies and lead a lucrative life filled with colorful characters; at least a simple car chase. I mean come on! But it never really seems to reach that point. Mike leaving and women *not* sleeping with me was as dramatic as it got.

My life was nothing like the movies except for maybe those French films where a guy sits in a room for 46 of the 113 minutes staring silently at the walls against an anguished voice-over.

There seems to be no great fireworks-laden resolution with . . . Her (I don't dare poke at its gigantic still body. It's sure to rise up and punish me for my latest romantic disaster). "We" seems to be heading for a very slow nursing home kind of coma death. Puncuated, perhaps, by an occasional emotional flare-up. I had love malaria.

Even now, the most dramatic nights (and it's pretty much always in the night and only in my head) are washed away by the sheer weight of the ensuing days and,

BOOM!

Time slips in another quantum leap forward and Thanksgiving's here and Time now becomes The Holidays in capital letters. It takes on a life of its own. Nostalgia runs rampant and people's expectations run a dangerous course. All are instantly wired to all the Christmases past and all the things that happened and all the family bogeymen and at the heart of Christmas is the longing. Tiny Tim mashing his nose against the toy shop window (whatever happened to Glyn Dearman? Did he ever make another movie?) is the Sword of Damacles that many live under in the weeks from November 20th to January 2nd. Kids hoping for certain gifts, poor parents fretting the gifts they can't buy, middle-class angst in the crush of shopping mall madness as you finally crack and buy the fuckin' tie for Uncle Gordie.

And then there's the Signifigant Other. Or maybe you've just started and the current seriousness level has yet to be agreed upon. Perhaps silent hopes lie like land mines out there in the strangely amped Holiday Mood.

And so the hope lives at Marco's Trattoria, despite the heavy rains and the fact it's dying a slow death. There's no denying. It's bleeding all over the place. Niko's worrying they're gonna let her go.

"You just watch. I'll be the first to go. The black chick goes first, unh-huh. Keep you and Maxie, but not ol' Niko. Shit."

I don't say anything to either Niko or to Marco when he asks for my "honest opinion." My honest opinion? You need to win the lottery worse than me, man. But what can you say? Can't we cling to our dreams to the bitter end? Sometimes that's all there is. Especially during The Holidays.

They even took out an ad. The good places never advertised, but Marco's was on the ropes. It was banking on The Holidays.

"That's when people eat out!" Marco declared to me with his usual "We're Number One" index finger raised skyward.

"Oh, yeah," I told him. "When I worked at Saxon's we'd get slammed on Christmas and New Year's."

Marco's face lit up at the possibilities and by some fluke the bell rang, announcing the mistaken entrance.

"A customer!" and Marco was out of the kitchen to greet the first new customers of our latest change-for-the-better business.

e-mail

I went home and turned on the computer, avoiding in one fell swoop social contact, masturbation and old movies. In my mailbox was an exciting letter. My first E-mail from Mike. It came from a town somewhere north of Prague. It came from a land where they call beer *pivo*.

Subject:
   Hey man. It's all good
Date:
   Fri, 28 Nov 1997 15:02:06 +0100
From:
   MacIlvie@antik-fryc.cz

Yo dude!

Have you ever gotten an e-mail from the Czech Republic, motherfucker!! No fucking way, bitch! Man it is a fucking trip and cold as hell! And get this, the beers are 40 cents for a half-liter which is like a pint. 40¢!! Dinner costs about $2 for a plate of goulash and dumplings. They eat a lot of dumplings here.
And the women!! They're tall and beautiful and my buddy tells

me they're all good to go. There are three or four fine ass bitches in every one of my classes. Oh, dude I can't wait. I feel like a new man.

I'll tell you more later as I gots to go.

Late,

M

the return of the north county girl

The North County Girl called again out of nowhere and considering that absolutely no other women were on my horizon (and I'm high atop the main mast scanning, scanning ever vigilantly the horizon from the crow's nest with very powerful binoculars. Nothing) I agreed to a date. We had gone out a few times back in September sometime between Nurse! (if the North County Girl would have slept with me I might have been guilty of cheating) and Anastasia, but on the romance front (what *she* calls the romance front, but which I like to think of as the sex front) our dates had a Prozac overdose energy to them. So after about three of those special dates, the appearance of an exotic Russian intellectual and a couple of messages on our respective answering machines, the North County Girl and I seemed comfortable with never again speaking to each other ever. Until today, when she rings me up with perfect timing.

I think it's The Holiday Syndrome. Perhaps she has momentarily dropped her standards or thrown caution to the wind in order to at least have a man around during the crucial period from mid-November to January 1st.

It happens sometime around daylight saving time or standard time, whatever the fuck the clock "falls back" to at the end of

October. In a day the days are far shorter. Darkness comes quicker and is longer-lasting. The sun dips, the mercury plummets and The Holidays loom.

Sure, Halloween is a piece of cake and even a certified depressive can weather Veterans Day, but when the leaves begin to fall and the stores set up their window displays and our reliable and beloved chicken gives way to a nostalgic love of turkey, when there can be no denying that the fourth Thursday of November is coming up quick, well, you know where this road leads: the seven candles of the menorah, the twelve days of Christmas and, finally, New Year's Eve, the night no self-respecting woman wants to face alone.

Friends step up to aid the singles, but that's no good. A woman would like to be able to drag her very own man to Betty's Christmas party, even if it is a guy who can kill a conversation with a simple statement (any statement, it doesn't matter; that's his gift). But at least she can say she found him all on her own, at least none of her friends had to drag some wrecky bachelor in for an attempted setup that will never go anywhere but has the potential to ruin a ten-year-long friendship with Betty.

This syndrome only lasts 'til, say, the second or third week of January, when they wake from the malady. It happens right around the time that the Christmas tree begins to dry up and become a fire hazard. If it works out just right, you can take the tree out to the curb with you on your way out of their lives and if things are truly fair, the guy gets breakfast and sex that morning.

"What was that?" I'd forgotten I was on the phone with her. If I didn't get laid soon permanent ADD was bound to set in. My sexual flights of fancy were seeping into everything.

"I thought maybe we could go hiking or something. And then get something to eat!" It sounded so exciting.

"Sure, why not." I'd forgotten about her natural enthusiasm. "Let's do it!" I say, and so we do.

•   •   •

What the fuck, I don't have a thing. My stomach's sour, my brain aches, my mind bakes, my tongue is thick and my spit is foamy and it's very late and I'm back home after a waste of time with the North County Girl. We just sat around and bullshitted. Just threw a bunch of bullshit around like it's changing the fucking world. I bonded with her in fake enthusiasm, the Friday night bar enthusiasm I'm so well versed in.

But it was all bullshit anyway with her one little peck on the cheek to end our first date (which in reality is our fourth date). Is she kidding?! I guess not, for it's "Good night. I had a really fun time," she smiles and really seems to mean it. Then she's out the car, no invite up for "Something to drink?" Can we at least save our disappointment for coming down the stairs of her probably ratty little apartment 'cause what else the fuck could it be but some half-assed crap hole if they don't want me!? If they don't want me, well then fuck 'em and therefore their place must be a dump.

But I didn't get far enough to report on her housing situation. Boom! she was out the door with a kiss and a good night, so who the fuck cares?

Apparently me.

I drive home alone and vaguely disgruntled and decide that it's times like these that fuel the very world of monogamy: the drive home alone nights, the little peck on the cheek after whippin' out the MC for the meal beyond your means and it's still not enough. The standing with your buds sayin', Go up to her. Why don't you go up to her? You go up to her, you're the one that likes her dumbfoundedness, to all the nos, the get-losts, to all the snubs, the endless gentle brush-offs, to the girl who when you finally get her in that room at night . . . she just doesn't go, so close to all her naked delights and she still doesn't go. To all of that and the above not mentioned things but from the male perspective you know what I'm talking about, we salute:

MONOGAMY

Like a dim-witted ex-con, it's the best life we know and while we ache for our freedom we fall back with a sense of relief to our cell of monogamy.

But even I didn't believe such crap as I made my way through thick clouds and misty rain over yet another bridge back to my house that was love and juicy sex vacuum-empty. I try to make it this evil, soul-killing prison when they won't have me, but, really, when I'm alone, that special girl (a new one, an old one, my fantasy amalgamation) whom I can't help but dream on and the prison transform together into a warm loving land in the face of all the limitless coldness and disinterest that lies out there awaiting you. I dream about the girl that really *does* like you. The girl you really like.

I wondered if it might ever again happen to me. If I might squire a lovely down the lane, a woman whose sap begins to flow upon my touch, at the very thought of me, an actual excitement rather than a "Well, it was on sale" mentality. I don't know. I got nothing.

crab again

The wet weather was relentless. El Niño was colicky and would not be quieted. The basil and fresh farmers' market tomatoes had long ago faded and so we headed into the mushrooms and the roast meats with starchy polentas and risotto. The beets and leeks were beautiful and shiny in December and we used lots of them in salads and soups and don't forget the pumpkins and butternut squashes we roasted and put in giant ravioli that floated in duck stock with shaves of Reggiano.

I tried to fatten on this warm comforting fare at Marco's Trattoria that wet winter, El Niño placing a double curse on my rotten luck by soaking me and making me feel chill to the bone and reluctant to leave my solitary, warm and dry abode.

But despite El Niño, regardless of my Time-Life flow problems, the day came when the first catches of crabs arrived at the docks and then the fish markets. While word was they were not so plentiful, rumor had it that the ones caught in the crab traps were fat and fine. So one day I offered to take Gina to the Chinatown markets to pick up some bright and lively ones. While Gina knew all about the intricacies of southern Italian cuisine, I knew about the basement Oaktown Chinatown seafood shop.

We were driving in my car on the way to Chinatown. I'd never been with Gina outside of work and the first few minutes of silence were excruciating. And then she broke the silence and it felt even worse.

"So, you don't have a girl?"

"Hmmm?" I felt busted! Doesn't she know that in America we're more discreet about such things? On the way to buy crab one might ask, "Are you seeing anybody?" but not "So, you don't have a girl?" Jesus, get with it!

"Well, I'm not seeing anybody," I answered. "Right now."

She looked at me the same way she'd look at Niko when Niko wasn't ready on time. "Hmmm . . ." She seemed skeptical.

"None of them seem any good," I said. "I don't know . . ."

"Men."

"What?" I smiled. "What's that mean?"

She just shook her head and looked out the car window.

"Men? How 'bout women?" I asked.

"Women at least know what's worthwhile—not like men, sniffing around like dogs all the time." She looked at me for a moment. "Isn't this the street?"

We parked and toured the bustling Oakland Chinatown streets, checking out all the produce and fresh chickens and fish and lines of glistening red ducks hanging in the windows.

I saved for last my favorite shop, the store where you go down the wet concrete steps into the fishy-fresh smells of the basement market to see the tanks filled with coiling gray catfish, lobsters still in their murky green water, turtles that seem to almost huddle in their boxes as though more aware of their plight than the simple crustaceans and fishes. And then the two big tanks full of crabs. That's what we were after.

The Asian man in the white butcher's coat fished the scrambling creatures out of the big tank. The crabs were the same all over town, like they had come out of a press, but Gina was sharp-eyed and made sure all were quite kicking and missing no legs; that's the main thing. You don't want to buy a gimpy crab.

Our dream was to drop them into pots of boiling water. If there were enough of them you'd have to hold the lid on for a minute with a towel wrapped round your hand to protect yourself from the heat the crabs scrambled and kicked against. The lid would bounce and clack from their struggle for a minute maybe and then all was still in the roiling water. After about ten minutes remove the lid and there's that baby shit green foam and the brackish ocean smell of boiled crab.

It was going into ravioli. Gina was almost disgusted by the idea, it was so nouvelle. Where she came from they had not our amazing Dungeness and so they developed few recipes for sweet fresh crab and Gina was lost in her role as the staunch traditionalist.

Maxie, Niko and I were picking over all those crabs, now boiled and steaming brinely on the prep table. We were talkin' and jokin' in Spanish and in English, taking bites of the crab now and then. We boiled one extra, the one "for the pot," Gina said; that was us. We were the pot. Niko liked that body meat while I went for the fattest joint of the fattest leg as the oyster of my eye. Meanwhile, Maxie was systematically piling up the red fibrous claw meat and I finally figured he had some antojito in mind so I threw into his pile.

"Está bien?"

"Sí!"

"Qué vas preparar?"

"Solo tacos con salpicón." Maxie shrugged like it wasn't anything to get excited over.

"What's Max makin'?" Niko asked.

"Tacos. Probably onion, cilantro, chile . . ."

"Put me down with that." Niko tossed a handful of body meat to the pile. "I want some of that."

e-mail

Subject:
  Yo Yo Ma
Date:
  Thur, 4 Dec 1997 15:02:06 +0100
From:
  MacIlvie@antik-fryc.cz

Dude, the following is true and I can't believe how soon. I just fucking got here. I was at the school where I teach, doing my theater class, which ran a little late. I had been flirting around with this girl.

The best looking one in the class, her name is Katka, KATKA, Kaaatkaaa. Mamma. We had taken some props out of the library, and as everyone was leaving, I asked if anyone would help me. Of course, I voiced this as anyone, but Katka is pretty much the only one within hearing range. My bosses had left and we are putting this shit up, joking around.

She was wearing this little skirt. I don't know how these Czech girls can wear those things in the winter, but I ain't complainin'. So I'm thinking, naturally, this has all the potential of a fantasy in the making. So, Pow. Move a little closer, talk a

159

little softer. What are you doing tonight? I don't know. Do you have to be somewhere soon? No. Perfect, perfect. When I bust the move, she's all into it. I fucking hiked up that little skirt of hers, placed her wee arse on a desk and tore it up. In the Library. Yeah, boy. Hands down the sexiest Czech words: To byl nelepshi orgasmus. (That was the best orgasm).

I love teaching. I love studentkas. I cannot believe how fucking horny these girls are.

By the way, I still don't have my address, I will get it soon, but I just wanted to let you know I nailed that chick. And I nailed IN THE SCHOOL, IN THE LIBRARY, and I AM gonna nail her again. Hot Damn. You know it makes me think about going back. I'm gonna go back to the fucking states, and I'm gonna have to deal with all these fucking uptight American "don't touch me that's harassment" bitches, back into the neurotic "Do you really love me?" bullshit, back into the constant conflicts, mind games, bickerings, competitions, and I'm not gonna get a single piece of pussy. Not one. I know it. And its gonna be some ugly fucking bitch when I do. I'm afraid to leave. How can I leave young beautiful willing pussy? How can a man bring himself to do such a thing?

These girls don't have the hang-ups, the emotional seesaws, the fucking having to be equal, having to be better, having to put you through tests and all that shit.

So what are you waiting for? Get your ass out here. I think one of the teachers is leaving in a couple of weeks. He misses his muthafuckin' mommy or some such shite.

M

torta pasquale

Wow! I was at the same time excited, relieved, jealous, sad, depressed and hopeful over Mike's fantasy fuck story. In the Czech Republic, no less! But my mind simply couldn't quite come to terms with my best friend taking a plane seven thousand miles to touch down in a country where he can't even speak the language and he gets laid before I do. Ah . . . ah. . . . ah . . . ! is all my brain can do in the end, so I turned my thoughts to the Torta Pasquale or I don't know that I'd have made it through the day.

Marco spoke of the Torta Pasquale in the most reverent of tones. As though it was a long-lost separated-at-birth twin he was soon to reunite with. The Torta Pasquale.

"Sixty-five centimeters across!" he would erupt at times so that no one could dare deny this magnificent torta.

I asked Gina that day to get my mind off.

"What's with this Torta Pasquale? Have you ever seen one?"

"It's a Genovese dish," she said with the begrudging respect she paid all but true Sicilian food. "It's big. . . . I guess the men are impressed with its bigness."

She made one the next day. A smaller one, maybe forty centimeters across, to fit in the oven. It was like a big filo-dough pie filled with light ricotta cheese and wilted chard and many layers.

There was nothing amazing about its flavor upon first bite, but it had a surprising comfort about it, as though you were restored a bit by eating it even though the flavors were muted.

It was a definite brown bagger. The type of food that profited from being carried around with you for a bit. Like Savarin's ripening partridge, it gained with time 'til you reached in, almost home, or late at night. Then! a bite of Torta Pasquale was marvelous indeed. Nearly as satiating as a young Czech woman that awaits you far away.

I left work still squeezeless but with a fat slice of the torta in my pocket dreaming of the fantasy girls (today it's Gina Gershon and hot Czech chicks in short skirts), plotting on how to sleep with my lone real-life girl, the North County Girl (I've placed Niko and the bread store girl I've been exchanging glances with for six years in the fantasy category for today). I'm doggedly determined to crack this nut (though my effort has a lame silver medal feel about it, seeing as my best buddy has already won the pussy race on an international level).

I walked home working up various nutcracking strategies. It was as though the North County Girl had become the only woman engaging in sex within driving distance (and remember, I've gone as far as fifty-five miles). All other women were happily married, gay or in a convent as far as I was concerned. The fact that she had allowed me to kiss her and fondled a breast on our last date somehow sealed it. I'd taken . . . what? Second base? Second base was mine, don't even try to take that away from me. With every other woman on the planet I was either already damaged and discarded goods (been there, done that) or I wasn't even up to bat. With every other woman there were still a million levers to pull, knobs to adjust, instrument-laden balloons to launch just to get to the point I was at with the NC Girl: walking home from work wondering how two people could be struggling so over sex like it was some toy which technically belongs to her and all I'm saying is, Wouldn't it be fun if we took it out of the box and played with it?

almost middle-aged man and the sea

I had that thing again this morning. That thing where I feel like I'm living on Jupiter or possibly Saturn. One of the fat assed planets. Gravity alone makes rising from the bed a near impossibility. It's just too much to bear. My meager frame feels like it's hauling a long ton. My brain operates under 6 atm. I walk across my room as though on the bottom of the Marianas Trench with the world's longest snorkel.

I had to finally give in and go back to sleep (on days off I require something on the order of ten hours of sleep). I'm trying to regain a dream wherein . . . She (Mrrower! Khaaaah! The monster spits like a cat now, attenuated by my sleepiness) is explaining to me her newfound lesbianism and then reveals the existence of a hotter younger sister I'd never known about.

I righted myself around noon, and walked down to the Bay toward the "house" of an old and dear friend whose company I could stomach three or four times a year. Actually, we've both somehow settled into an agreement on that frequency and in my mind this confirms again our friendship.

I wanted to see Chris because he's been in a bit of a rut as far as the opposite sex is concerned. I'm not really on a mission to cheer *him* up, it's *me* who'll feel better by hanging out with a man who measures his lonely days in years compared with my weeks. At least I was dating.

Chris's latest dry spell started just before the Democrats took over the White House (his slumps can be measured in presidencies; the last time Chris got laid Bush might have made the congratulatory call). His well went dry back then and, lately, he claims to have no interest or desire to even continue with the exploratory drilling anymore, but then, he does live in a dilapidated boat tied to a scuzzy dock, so it all kind of dovetails together nicely.

I stopped by the market because the first tangerines had arrived and I pictured sitting in Chris's "living room" listening to music, talking and drinking freshly squeezed tangerine juice first and then moving on to the tangerine screwdrivers as the conversation deepened. It was at the produce market that I ran into an old flame.

Let's call her . . . Claudia. I'd seen her just three weeks prior. I'm sure it was her. It'd been a few years but people don't change that much or, certainly, total strangers don't change into someone who looks exactly like someone you once knew. So I knew it was her. But in my strangeness of two months ago that persists to varying degrees to this day, I was unable to approach her. She stood two people deep in a parallel checkout line universe and I looked her way two or three times and got the distinct impression that she was avoiding eye contact.

But today it couldn't be avoided and I was bold enough to break the silence. It happened in the potato section. I was deciding between the Russian fingerlings, the banana fingerlings, the ruby crescents or the Yukon "Bs." I chose the Russians despite their prohibitive price because they're magnificent and I love nothing more than a fine creamy tuber. Buying a "Russian" would also lend credence to my claim that I held no grudge against Anastasia.

That's when Claudia approached. She was pushing a shopping

cart that bore various bags of produce and what looked like one of those Romanian babies that used to be quite popular for adoption. The baby was wearing what appeared to be clothing designed for an infant Dalai Lama topped with a multicolored and—I'm fairly certain—hand-sewn crown or kaffiyeh; I can never tell those two apart.

"Oh, my god, Carl? Is that you?" were her first words after my "Claudia . . . ?"

It turned out the kid was hers and not the love product of war-torn peasant borscht eaters. The child seemed content and curious in a drooling sort of way, but its forehead distracted me as Claudia and I caught up on our lives.

I told her about still working in a kitchen like it had the stink of failure all over it while glancing repeatedly at the baby's head. What's with that forehead? Is it fucking protruding? It's protruding. Even for a baby that's protrusion (*wasserkopf*, my aunt would call it), but seeing as I'm almost never within a hundred yards of anyone under drinking age I have to admit that I'm no toddler phrenologist so I tried to let the kid's misshapen head go as Claudia described the contentedness (that seemed to come with a heaping helping of boring) of her married life, but that kid's head?! I don't know.

It turns out Claudia married the guy (who had a bit of a pro-truding forehead, now that you mention it) who was her sort-of boyfriend when we had our sort-of affair. Unbeknownst to Claudia this has added another notch to my belt. The belt signifying women hurled headlong into marriage soon after sleeping with me. It now stands at five. Something's up. Perhaps it's a career opportunity. Men could hire me to finalize their wedding plans. A couple of weeks before popping the question just let me take your would-be-fiancée out for an evening and she'll scurry back to her apartment, double-lock and bolt that door, pull the sheets up to her chin and see you in a whole new light. You can now rest assured that when on bended knee the answer to your hopes and dreams will be a resounding "Yes!"

I headed on with a bag of tangerines now, wrestling with my feelings about marriage. These feelings were complicated by the fact that I didn't even have a woman. The danger being that, in this alone state, marriage seemed fucking fantastic. Claudia was nice. She'd've made a great companion and this North County Girl seems to live and breathe this family picket fence shit. Ahh, wedded bliss. Maybe . . . ?

Unfortunately, whenever I *was* sleeping with a woman I felt about marriage the way many girlfriends have felt about anal sex— it's kind of intriguing, but just a little too scary. Could pleasure *really* be realized through that route?

Chris and I have had a couple glasses of simply smashing fresh tangerine juice and we're already at work on the screwdrivers. We've known each other since high school and both ended up in the Bay Area from down by the border. We have that easy comfortableness of long-standing friends.

We're sitting in what Chris likes to call his living room, but which most nautically minded people probably classify as the bilge. Chris has his latest compilation tape on his jerry-rigged boom-box sound system: Bands That Were Famous for Five Minutes. It isn't very good since all the five minutes are now over and after a bit of initial excitement with 4 Non-Blondes and the Knack it becomes downright sad so we switch to Mahler's First and turn it down.

"You're losing your hair, aren't you?" Chris asks with the genuine concern bushy-haired men wield so effortlessly. It's pretty much the first thing he's brought up since an "Oh, wait 'til you hear the latest tape I made; this one's great!" upon my arrival. I'm surprised it took this long for his first shitty comment. He likes to insult me in a random manner. It's why I only see him three or four times a year. Chris is like a dessert wine, tolerable only in the smallest doses.

He looks me intently in the eye or, more accurately, past my eyes to the back of my head. He seems to lean toward me as though to get a better look at some top rear scalpal region that my eyes can only see through the use of the dangerous Two Mirrors Trick that I haven't dared again perform since a traumatic mishap with it four days after . . . She left.

I realize that my hair isn't all it might be. I'm not one of the lucky ones who have hair that lies like a beaver pelt on their head well into their forties. I've already passed the point of being de- scribed as "boyish." Maybe my hair *is* the source of my sex/love/ women problems. Maybe it's not my personality or job. Fuck!

"They got this drug that'll make your hair grow back," Chris explains.

"Yeah, Rogaine. Thanks for your help."

"No, this other shit that really works."

"Mmmm . . ." I'm getting sour, I can feel it.

"It's a pill," he explains, "but there's a problem with dizziness, high blood pressure, sleeplessness . . ." He says this as though he's got the fucking prescription for me.

"That's . . . interesting," I say, hoping he'll fucking get off it already.

". . . and impotence!" Chris says it with glee that I perceive mo- mentarily as a cheer for the net hard-cock loss that would result and I wonder, What *is* his game?

"Oh, come on!" I'm getting pissed off now. Why is he so anti- Carl-gets-laid anyway?

"Yeah, I'm serious." He won't stop. "The FDA is approving the shit, can you believe that?"

"It makes your hair grow back but you can't get it up anymore?" I ask.

"Well, fifteen to thirty percent don't."

"Don't what? Grow hair or get it up?"

"I forget which. Is that a trip, though? Would you use it, huh?"

"I don't need it!" I protest.

"Maybe not yet, but, wouldja? If you hadta? Hmmm?"

I think about it for a minute and imagine having some amazing Cesar Romero head of hair. The kind of shit you find on rain forest natives 300k up the Amazon. That paintbrush shit. But then if I couldn't get it up what would be the point? I'd be sitting around my living room with this amazing hair wondering what to do with myself. All of a sudden there'd be lots of time.

I figure enough of this hair shit. I drain my tangerine screwdriver and decide to put Chris back in his place and visit again sometime in the spring. "I saw this chick the other day, looked just like Pernilla. Remember her?"

Chris lets out a sigh as he often would, and we've known each other for so long that his sigh is worth a thousand words to me. Pernilla is the woman that brought on Chris's still-active rut. It began the day Pernilla finally left him and returned to the land of dill and the midnight sun. Scandinavia.

Pernilla was this six-foot blonde Amazon au pair (and this was before the au pair thing got out of hand, scoring for Pernilla even more unneeded hot-sex bonus dividend points). Pernilla was as pretty as could be with amazing teeth for a European and one look at her tight heart-shaped ass stuffed into those faded Guess? jeans left many a man ready to dash themselves upon the rocky shores of love and lust's utter hopelessness.

No one could really believe that Chris had stumbled upon such a mother lode honeypot of Scandinavian flesh because he *never* got any. He could barely keep a job. Good luck pretty much avoided

Chris most of his adult life. It was why I was sitting in the bilge wondering how long it takes moisture to seep through a complete *New York Times* Sunday paper I was using as a cushion.

One day, many moons ago, he came home, from a Tribe Gathering no less, his arm around a tall hot blonde with an accent. Pernilla would greet us in a not-that-long T-shirt every morning (I could smell the fucking sex on her half the time!) for the next eleven weeks.

The household was thrown into a near sexual funk that entire summer. We were practically in an uproar, fomenting over our sex jealousy. Chris's import woman made all of our respective "rides" seem like ten-year-old AMC Pacers with crumpled passenger doors held together by complex bungee cord systems. Thinking about it too hard could short-circuit your brain like one of those out o' control Japanese animes.

It was bullshit. If it wasn't her fucking ABBA tapes it was the sex noises coming out of his room most every afternoon. And let me tell you, nothing quite gnaws at you while you're sitting woman-free on the couch as does a hot woman's *accented* groans coming from your roommate's bedroom. Her "ohs" jumped a register at the end: oh-ah! oh-ah! It was so European. I could almost see the blonde pigtails flying and her long Swedish legs pointing skyward.

Chris strutted about in the morning (which to this day means sometime around noon for him) like he was Joey Silvera or something. He even began a crash course in the study of Swedish to impress Pernilla (despite his happens-all-the-time-to-a-guy-like-me look, right off Chris was trying to glue himself to the rest of Pernilla's life as quickly and as permanently as possible).

His study began well enough with a cassette tape set that included a bilingual version of a Harold Robbins novel, but within fifteen minutes of putting on the headphones he was either valiantly fighting off sleep or had the bong bubbling furiously.

Of course, it couldn't last. Even back then Chris was already talking about living on a boat (I think at first Pernilla mistook this fantasy as involving travel, but Chris's boat was never going anywhere and despite the cultural and language differences she eventually figured this out). Besides, Pernilla had an entire other country to return to, with men who were even taller than her and who spoke her native tongue. He never had a chance.

It's because of that affair, followed by a few more years of bad dates and bungled semirelationships, that Chris ended up in a dilapidated boat and gave up on the exploratory drilling. Lost love, getting one's hands on a woman way above your league, had taken its toll. He ended up like one of the Coreys. Feldman, preferably.

As we sat (crouched or hunkered would be more accurate) in the bilge sipping our one-too-many fresh tangerine screwdrivers, Chris exhaled another grand sigh made all the more poignant (or pathetic, depending on how much tangerine-screwdriver-inspired milk of human kindness fills one's crankcase) by the creaking and groaning of his houseboat, which seemed to strain at the moorings like a dog that longed for a life beyond that which its master was willing or able to afford.

I was reminded of *Old Man and the Sea* right then. Spencer Tracy, my #1 Most Overrated Actor of All Time. But I did love him in *Old Man and the Sea*. Chris is like the Old Man to my four-tangerine-screwdriver reality. Chris is much younger, it's a wash on their hair, but the Old Man had the far better boat, not to mention a more "can-do" attitude. It's Chris's *life* that's tied to the boat all shark-mangled. It's goin' nowhere. Making compilation tapes seems to be Chris's current adventure.

north county girl, date #9

I'm deep in the middle of my weekend, encouraged by my near-stud classification in comparison to Chris. Tonight another date is scheduled and, as I explained earlier, I've taken second base with the North County Girl and she'd better not question me about that. If she even tries to take away second base I'm gone and I think that she senses this because when we finally got down to the couch (I await the girl on the couch like a child counting down the days until Christmas) she acts nearly eager for a little fun. And why not? It's Saturday night (I've even bribed Rock'n'Rollero to trade with me. This is costing me next Tuesday and a night to be named in the future along with a joint of sticky green, not to mention having to speak to him! I had to endure a rapier-like " 'Nother blind date?" from him, his first words to me since "Fuck you" so long ago. This girl has no idea how much she means to me).

It's late, it's her place and her possibly agoraphobic roommate has finally fucking vacated the premises by some minor miracle. Dinner's finished (it was a perfectly medium-rare steak au poivre with roasted walnut-sized red Norland potatoes and chard. But dessert was a disaster. I'd made some amazing fresh-out-of-the-oven palmiers and—I'm sorry!—store-bought ice cream because I cannot track down a good used ice cream maker and she tells me, "Ohhh, I can't eat dairy; I'm sorry," and she feels really bad, but it's true).

We got past the rapids of the dessert disaster, the bottle of Rhône wine is nearly gone, the talks have been talked, the meaningful moments realized, the laughs laughed, the glances exchanged and innuendo's foundation has been carefully laid as far as I'm concerned. I'm about as subtle and delicate as a man can be after forty days without a taste. There's nothing else left so I lean in for a kiss and the moment carries with it (in the all-important *my* mind) implications that had my breath nearly caught up in the top of my chest. My throat thickens, I lick my lips and lean in for what I'm hoping is the Quantum Leap Kiss.

She gives me one nice warm one and then,

Sha-Kack!!

A hidden team of her lawyers appear from the back of the apartment bearing briefcases and waving papers in my face. A cadre of life and house insurance experts, preschool admissions staffers, accountants and medical specialists concerned with my DNA have plenty of hard questions for me and if "her people" aren't happy with the answers "my people" can provide, well, boy, you just better be happy if I even let you slip that tongue in my mouth and allow those grubby financially challenged hands to fondle my full ripe breasts.

We're now in deep negotiations involving third base (if I had the connections I'd phone up Jimmy Carter and rent out Camp David in an attempt at reaching some sort of piece accord). One minute it was a date and the next a Starr Council has set up shop and the last thing I want is a Starr Council asking tough questions when all I'm thinking about is what fun we could have with her pussy and my cock. What a combination!

"I want to go a little slower," she says, like why can't I just understand (she almost seems to know that I've heard this line before). "I don't want to bond with someone and not have it work out." She looks at me pleadingly.

I nod like I'm right there with you, babe, thinking, *My kingdom for a horny girl!* as another thirty-something woman employs the stiff-arm on me. They wear their ovaries and life plans on their sleeves, these girls. They've Rip Van Winkled through their twenties (word has it they'd fuck men on a whim or a wave of alcohol-induced lust back then. In this cold wet thirty-something winter I can barely remember such glory days) and come to their senses a couple of months before meeting me.

"I want to have kids someday, you know?"

I nod. I've heard of this thing called children.

"It's an entire lifestyle. . . ." She seems to be testing me but it sounds more like a warning.

That's the problem. My "lifestyle" is only figured as far as to-morrow morning, while she's formulating Life Plans. The women are operating at a Graduate Level far beyond my Tits and Ass First Grade Primer. They're way past this silly passion-ruling-the-moment thing. Where has that gotten them? They'll tell you if you ask. They'll list the losers and creeps who've sullied their past, taken the prime of their youth, broken their delicate hearts.

I can tell she's sniffing me out. That's what probably shut it down the first time. I saw her for the drawn-out seduction that she was and she suspected me for the *Pussy First!* hound that I was.

So now we sit across from each other and it's gotten serious. My cheeks flush. The game's changed, at least for her. My cock screams the song that remains the same (I'm dying here, please dear God touch it—the tip, the tip; if this thing does not penetrate the moist realms of your garden of delights by Christmas I'll be the guy with the deer rifle in the clock tower). But the girl, now a full-grown woman, is thinking, I've got five years left at best. My ovaries ache to be fertilized. A few hundred good eggs have already been lost (perhaps one or two accidentally impregnated, only to be aborted in quiet shame) and if you're not going to use these eggs properly then I might just have to close up the egg shop entirely.

It's an impasse that even Henry Fonda in *Twelve Angry Men* couldn't overcome. While I'm still thinking, She seems nice enough, great (insert body part here). Cool, she's thinking, This guy better be fucking serious for I have not a single minute to waste on simple boudoir frolicking in my holy quest for the man who will complete my life and father my child (maybe children—I haven't quite decided). If his W-2 checks out and he gets along with his mother only then can he complete my picture and I can turn to my sisters and say, "See? I *can* procure a desirable mate who shall defend the home from small sounds in the night, repair minor household appliance breakdowns and if not fix the car at least talk to the mechanic."

"I like you" is my monster Oliver Wendell Holmes summation of my own emotional state and expectations grid, even though I'm unsure even of this declaration and the more she mentions kids the less sure I get. I stroke her arm and my mouth screams for a kiss. "Haven't we had fun?"

"Yeah, I like spending time with you. You're funny and nice," she says, and it seems enthusiastic and true for once. That she likes me. "But, I don't know, what do you want to do with your life? I'm trying to figure out what I want to do. . . . You know? It's not like we're twenty anymore. I want to have the things I want to have."

I'm stunned. Deep down I know what she's saying, but tonight I only want a kiss. I don't want to feel like time is of the essence. I'm not ready to think about my life having some sort of a shelf life. That there's an expiration date. Well, I know about death. That expiration I have well-formulated in my mind and it still seems far off enough to remain unfrightening. It's the living breathing still walking without a cane expiration date I'm talking about. That possibly decades-long "too late" portion of Life. For instance, 100-meter dash medalist? Right. Poet? Too old—they're typically washed up in their twenties. Complete and utter career change to, say, flight traffic controller? Not according to the look on the face of the guy in the flight tower who looks at my resume and says, "But you're a cook!" And that takes us, or me at least, to women.

I always imagined that it would never be too late to have a woman, a lover, even a lifelong mate, but it's different now. There are hurdles and qualifications. A bit of job interview has slipped into the mix. In my late teens I could mention to a little cutie that I was thinking about being in a band and that was enough ("Oooh, really?" was a typical enthusiastic exclamation). In my twenties, fine, I had to at least have a guitar lying about and be able to struggle through the tricky A to D to E chord change, but the dream alone still carried with it some weight. But now? In my thirties? They want proof, documentation, personal references.

"Are you in a band now?" she'll not be at all shy about asking.

"Well, er . . ."

"Have you even played in a band . . . ever?"

"Hmmm . . ."

"It says here you were with . . . Sheila, is it?"

"Yeah . . ."

"You were with Sheila from March of '92 to the summer of '93?"

"Yeah, about that."

"Well, that leaves quite a gap between her and Dolores who you claim to have been monogamous with from February '87 to January '88. What were you doing from January of '88 to the spring of '92?"

"Uh . . . single?" See? I've already lost. I'm not husband material.

The lack of any sort of a record contract or CD and the disturbingly short Dolores "relationship" prove that.

It seems that tonight a winning smile, quick quip and perfectly medium-rare steak will only get me so far with the North County Girl. Exactly how far I'm still trying to figure out but I'm guessing that digital penetration is probably out.

Luckily my credit rating and my platform position on children ("They're nice!" I say as though Barry Sheck has finally badgered it out of me. "Do you *want* kids?" She's dogged. "*Someday.*" It's an admission, not a life's mission, she can see this) still rates a slumber party complete with gentle breast fondling, two or three minutes of kissing complete with tongues (and possibly a brief instance of heavy breathing on her part, though this might be merely a ruse of hers to force me to go out and get a better job) and some light ass caressing (and let me say, the torture was exquisite. Her full breasts, soft skin, wonderful smell and smooth round bottom could only have been a test by a perverse god telling me: "Let go of the pussy, boy, and I shall show you a world of true spiritual delight. There are worlds beyond the pussy, my son!" But I didn't listen).

Instead I spent the first thirty minutes under the sheets playing gently with her (and, I'd just like to go on record to say that "I'm sleepy!" even when said with the utmost cheer are just not the words a man wants to hear when he's dialing away on a woman's stiffened nipples like a safecracker under deadline pressure), then three or four minutes of quiet huffs and sighs and back turns to let her know of my displeasure at the lack of cock attention I was getting followed by a forty-five-minute mental rundown on women I *have* fucked.

I awoke covered in a light sweat. Full morning light filled the room and the NC Girl was lying beside me sweet and asleep as a little girl, a soft tender woman in my arms. My scoundrel fantasy—

the bitter pill stuck in my craw—could just barely glimpse it as such as it took place in real time. I couldn't, even in the hopeful potential light of a new morning, appreciate the innocent tenderness that brought a sleeping smile to her face as I stroked her wonderful shoulder and she murmured and snuggled closer to me as though I were a wonderful life-affirming thing.

"I'll make you some coffee!" She was now smiling and jumped out of bed, her breasts filling the satiny nightie that shimmered in the morning light, a false promise I no longer believed in.

I drove away that day in a mild funk, the lengthening length of my time out of the saddle almost resigning me. The thing they never figured, the part the women couldn't get, was the pressure cooker nature of the male psyche.

I think a quick blow job is the better way to keep a guy strung along until the woman's made up her mind. It would be like the lottery, or Vegas. An occasional big payoff. Everybody knows that's the best way to keep the rat tugging at the lever. If it's always "no" I'll end up sulking in my rat corner feeling bad about the lever.

und keine eier

Subject:
  And no eggs
Date:
  Wed, 10 Dec 1997 15:52:29 +0100
From:
  MacElvie@antik-fryc.cz

I am back in the pussy saddle again. It comes in seasons and it comes in winter and it comes in Czech!! I got this little hottie (yes, a new one!) to give up the head INSIDE a shitter stall, while in the next stall this man was taking an extremely loud fart-filled shit. How's that for entertainment?! Well, girlie girl didn't let flatulation and the splash of fecal matter deter her and the mission was accomplished. I got another date with this girl this Friday. I went on two with her already, and got her hot and bothered, so this date is what you could call a meet at the pub, leave instantly and go fuck kinda date. Should be fun. She's quite young, but I'm startin' to acquire a taste (17!). Aint so bad.

Speaking of young freshies. My friend and I were talking about the finer points of doing young girls, and I said, "You know, they're just so fresh," and he says, "Yeah they are fresh when you get them, but then when you're through with them, they look like a bulldog that just got done eating porridge." British humour.

I moved to this country and became a pig. Oh, well, Take it easy, man.

M

night and day

I turned off the computer completely discouraged. I could neither fall for a girl properly nor just have my way with one and here Mike seemed to be getting laid like a fucking maniac. I'm sure at least some of it was true though Mike *was* the guy I'd followed through neighborhoods in the City in search of mythical parties beyond anything imaginable, rooms filled with women and cocktails, cool guys you hadn't seen for a while and more women. "Wait'll you see," he'd tell me. Then we'd spend the whole night and up until dawn traipsing through town and finding parties and wrong addresses and ending up in some bar usually with two guys, friends we'd run into or sometimes a party that soon melted down to three or four people (all guys), a sputtering keg of watery beer, never any chicks or the few you'd see were from out of town and sniffing at you suspiciously.

But I knew some of it was true and it made me ache jealously. It made me resent the NC Girl and dream of exciting flights overseas. My entire being hovered over nasty and frequent carefree sex and tender love. The gutter or the heavens were all I'd have right then.

la doña and the white-haired lady

It was Monday, an easy lunch shift and so a very beloved day. I'm coastin' to the weekend. It's the usual slow lunch. So we're working in the kitchen, not much to do and I'm thinking, Okay, maybe Mike isn't the go-to guy when it comes to advice about the ladies. So far he's had me tell a woman to go and fuck herself and he's set me up with an emotional train wreck chick who I was on Love's third-story ledge with. Now he's ditched his woman and gone off to the Czech Republic where, apparently, amazing sex grows on trees. Where has that left *me?'*

So I asked Niko what it is exactly that a woman looks for in a man, and she told me.

"Well, I ain't no white woman. They want to know all about your job, how much money you make, what kinda car you drivin' . . ."

"Exactly!" I agreed. She knows; she has that natural earthy sense that I grant women of color. "It's like a job interview."

"Thank you. No, unh-unh, I just want a man that got a job, you know? Treat his woman right. I guess that's what I'm lookin' for, a man who will treat a woman right," she said as though this were the first time she'd come to this heartfelt conclusion.

"And how is that?" I asked, not sure that men knew how to do that.

"I don' know, but ya know when ya found it. Calls you up and says he's been thinkin' about you, that's always nice. Says he misses you. Listens to you when you talk. You can mostly tell by his friends and how he treats his family."

"Hmmm . . ." I can use a phone, but *I've been thinking about you*? I don't know, I mostly think about myself and I only miss things that are actually gone. My family I don't even want to get into and now that Mike's gone I have no friends. This isn't looking good.

"Now, if you wanna know the turnoffs, that I can be even more specific about."

"Oh, yeah?" I'm now eager, hoping she won't mention hair. Then I'll have broken even on this exchange.

"Yeah, little hands, tiny feet? Unh-unh. Pants too short with the socks slippin' under his heels? Brings a pee-chee folder with poems on your second date?! He thinks these poems will finally convince you 'bout poetry. Flowers . . ."

"Flowers are bad?"

"On the first date?!"

"Oh."

"Has these trips planned, these amazing trips . . . to places you hate! Like . . . Reno! And then he spends five hours at the nickel slot machine until Wayne Newton's show, talkin' about the great buffet at Circus Circus; 'They're gonna have those special rolls. . . .' " Hih-hih-hih, Niko laughed; she had the greatest laugh. "Damn."

"Sounds like somebody in particular."

"Pitiful Phillipe. I fell for that dang French accent. He ended up being like Kaczynski except he wasn't smart enough to make bombs. Had the lights on while we're gettin' wicked."

"Lights are bad?"

"Well, maybe one. A candle's cool, but he had the overhead on, bed lamp, candles, flashlight, like he ain't ever seen a naked woman and he don't want to miss a thing."

"See, you should just go out with me."

"You never asked." Niko smiled and walked out the kitchen, leaving me alone no further down the road of figuring things out than before.

I decided to ask the beacon of positive light energy, Ramona, what the fuck is going on.

"Ramona, what's the secret for you and Red?"

"Who?" she asked like "What the fuck?"

"Your boyfriend. Red. He's cool." I was now Mister Sunshine with Ramona. "How do you guys do it?"

"Oh, the asshole?"

"Hmmm?"

She marched out the door into the dining room.

I got to the bottom of it when she came back.

"I finally realized he was too materialistic." It was the only time I'd seen Ramona look bitter. "He came off all spiritual, but he only cared about money."

"What'd he become a waiter?"

"You're so negative. Remember, healing starts with you. No, I caught him in bed with a numerologist. Some slut with a folding table and chair on Telegraph." Ramona walked out to the dining room, leaving me in the kitchen with no more answers than when I started, awaiting the arrival of two elderly ladies who lunch at Marco's every Monday. La Doña and the white-haired lady.

They walk in slowly, Doña guiding the older white-haired lady, who always wears the classic thin white sweater over her dowager's hump. La Doña spoke no English and the white-haired lady spoke no Spanish but they seemed the best of friends and, I suppose, spoke in a combination of telepathy and hand signals, intuiting the other's point or merely basking in the warm fuzzy melding of their life forces I think is how Ramona explained it to me like it was as obvious as shit.

They always ordered the same thing. The white-haired woman had the mild coppa sandwich with green salad for the side while La Doña always had the sirloin paillard, cut paper-thin and cooked well-done over the hot grill, salsa verde on top with some polenta, just a little, and extra vegetables. I took her order the first few times—Marco was gone and Ramona spoke no Spanish so she asked me to decipher the "Mexican woman's" order.

Doña's voice is a high thin distant Spanish. In any other register or language it might have been a monotone, but in La Doña it was musical. The other woman only pointed at the menu and in fact never even really looked up at me, but La Doña seemed pleased that I knew what she wanted and thanked me in her lilting quiet soprano. She even took to sending three dollars back to the kitchen as a tip every Monday that we divided up, Niko, Maxie and me.

Today I was hot on my fact-finding mission and so I walked out to the dining room and up to La Doña who could speak only Spanish and ignored her friend who could speak only English and I asked Doña in my pitiful Spanish,

"Digame de la Amor. Qué quieren las mujeres?"

"Ahh, la Amor." She smiled nostalgically and gently patted my forearm. "La primera cosa a entender de la Amor es. . . ." Her high thin monotone voice was magical and enigmatic and I was lost in the translation as she spoke of respect and companionship, something about truth in the heart and blood and then a bunch of words I couldn't understand that I imagined as the most important, most powerful clues, the long-lost keys to answer the riddle of my heart, but when she ended with a "Who can say?" I walked back into the kitchen unenlightened, though I did have the usual three dollars she always insisted upon.

She wouldn't take no for an answer. The three dollar bills were the crumpled many-folded variety that people with little money carry. I'd always take mine home and put them in a jar. It was money that I saved, money that had lost its cloak of anonymity. I knew where these bills came from. I'd seen the hands and purses of their previous owner. They were powerful dollar bills from the wise thin wrinkled old hand of La Doña and I saved them in a glass jar.

freak

So I hit a freak, okay? I wasn't just a lame pseudo serial monogamist this year of El Niño, this year of the Scoundrel. I took the information I'd garnered on Love and Women, La Doña's pure enigmatic advice, applied my recent experiences and went out and hit on this freak. It doesn't matter the details, just know it was late and I just couldn't fucking stand it one more night and I got lucky.

There was a damn it's late closing time desperate air about it (at least on my part). Like, go for it why don't you go for it she's not that hot but she's good to go just fuck her and be on your way isn't that what you're supposedly after? It was times like these that I could practically hear a voice in my head goading me on, "Do her! She wants it. Fuck her." Just remember, slap on the jimmy cap or be a foolhardy idiot who sweats AIDS in the middle of the night and drags themselves for a gut-wrenching test six months later swearing, Never again, never again.

So I decide to go for it. I wasn't even that attracted to her and she's probably thinking the same about me, I don't know. My empathy ended somewhere in my pants that night. But it's 2 A.M.; there, I'll admit it (a party would have had too many witnesses; this was anonymous bar closing shit. She can forever deny it and I'll tell my friends how hot she was).

As we entered her apartment my being swelled up to an amazing size. My larger than life Life was near bursting. I'd hit CEM. Critical Existential Mass. A hyper-self-consciousness that, to a Hindu, is as far away from Nirvana as spiritually possible.

The entire atmosphere rubbed me the wrong way. I walked in like I was robbing the place, like I was some sort of Ted Bundy dressed as a Jehovah's Witness. Her perfume, her fucking cigarettes, that laugh. What was I doing here? I'm not even that into it.

I was so full of myself that I near felt my fingers swell and become ever so slightly puffy and I sank into her saggy couch like I was made of lead.

We started to drink. It was the best plan.

And for a while, after enough drinking and the closing of eyes or the extreme darkening of the lights, once we decided fuck it! and started going at it, once we let the sex energy go, then there was something. A slightly devilish something, but that made it both good and bad.

And she did get nasty. She was a right little slut, though no matter how nasty she got, there was something false about the whole thing. But later, reflecting back on it all, the nastiness was great!

But before later, I drove home feeling like some cheap reluctant slut rallying now and then on a long ride home (when the semirural far East Bay was black as pitch and the sky wide and open) with the crowing of some hot cocksman.

Fucked this chick I just met and then left.

Yeah.

That was my crow that I'd rally with every few miles for a few miles more 'til I ended up at home and turned the key and cracked open the door and both my place and my soul were as empty as ever (though I enjoyed my alone-on-my-own-couch-sex-taken-care-of state. I truly did feel comfortable, fresh from a fuck, the woman long gone).

Sex.

Love.

I couldn't figure it. I was so on the fence about my entire life that it was beginning to really piss me off.

pasta carbonara and sour grapes

It was finally cold enough so that Gina allowed me to make one of my own specialties: pasta carbonara. She felt the cream and bacon and egg and cheese was simply too much for the summer or fall, like wearing white after Labor Day. But it got cold finally like it will now and then when frigid air blows down from Alaska and the Bay looks frozen still and the Golden Gate stands out as brilliant as can be in the rare cold dry air this rain-soaked El Niño winter and the stocking caps and thick coats at last come out. When it's time for pasta carbonara.

I stepped inside the kitchen escaped finally from that last and final cold blast of air. Gina was there and I looked up shaking my head, it was damn cold, about to say her very words,

"Pasta carbonara." She had the bags of top-flight Martinelli pasta laid out. She granted me my wish in that way Gina had of seeming to be pissed off when she did something nice for someone. Her compliments were all begrudgingly admitted, like there was finally no denying. Like she had some tough bitch reputation to maintain.

Like many great dishes it's deceptively simple: some diced pancetta (I liked to add some smokier American bacon; don't try and tell me Americans aren't the bacon masters, pancetta or not), sauté it 'til near crisp and then some diced onion and wilt them a bit and a splash of white wine and then the cream, toss the pasta in the pan and toss it again in a bowl with an egg yolk and fresh parsley, top it with fresh black pepper and grated cheese. I couldn't wait to have some. My primi piatti of the night.

But then, no sooner was I content with a full belly of pasta than Rock'n'Rollero appears for his grill shift and gives me this look that I don't like one bit. It's not the usual "I hate you" look. We're over that by now and simply avoid any eye contact.

No, tonight he's walking around cocksure and even more full of himself than usual. He's passing out little postcards announcing the appearance of his band (it's apparently a sort of Big Gig, the opening act of four at the Hotel Utah on a Tuesday, January 2nd. I'm fairly certain it's been calculated to be the most dead day on the Gregorian calendar) to everyone but myself. Somehow, without saying anything, he draws silent attention to this fact. That I don't get an invite. That he hates me. He wants everyone to know.

As we work silently in the kitchen, setting up for service, I smell something rotten. That doo-rag he wears over his long ponytailed hair is set at a rakish angle that I'm sure is directed directly at yours truly and there's some sort of smirk on his face. Since we don't speak he can't come out and say it, whatever "it" is, but he's up to no good.

And then Amber comes in for the grueling napkin folding that makes up a waitress's side work and though she's never given me a single encouraging look or word or any sort of shred of anything beyond the most cursory civility, I work on some witty repartee with encoded sexual innuendo to troll with tonight. Like there's still hope for something developing between us.

Amber came into the kitchen at one point to inquire as to the specials. I'm still working on some great line (maybe I'll tell her how much she'll like the Pasta Carbonara; that's my Oscar Wilde Moment so far) when she walks up to Rock'n'Rollero and comes to life. "They" even share a look (all of a sudden they're a "they") and I realize a great disaster has taken place. Rock'n'Rollero has achieved panty access to Amber, the latest third waitress. The fucker!

She's all smiles for him ("Hi, Larry"—she might as well sing it—while her "Hi, Carl" seems to include an unspoken "poor guy"). It's clear—mucous membranes have been transgressed. It's what I'm dying for and all of a sudden I'm dying of embarrassment and jealousy and resentment and loneliness and unrequited love OD. And then I even think she's shot me some sort of look like he's been talking shit about me to her, mentioning the blind date. The thing with the freak seems cheap and lame and now that bacon and cream isn't sitting too well in my stomach anymore.

are you ray?

I was down in the dumps. I was home alone and didn't want to
call the North County Girl and get into a debate about relationships, so I stared out my bedroom window, sitting in a chair, watching the rain roll down the window, watching the trees bend and
shake, listening to the wind that moved them about. I let Time
move me about. To an especially bad moment. To one in particular.

It was the blackest night. January 27th, three weeks after . . .
She left. I was standing in the parking lot of a bust ass restaurant,
the Cantina, down in Carmel having just successfully interviewed
for the highest-paying job I would have ever had, $35-40 thou, but
I'd have to move from Berkeley. I'd have to move down to the
Monterey Peninsula which already had a sourness about it from a
different broken heart. My very first broken heart—my first love,
my first kiss, the first woman I ever lived with—that handed me
a few short blocks from here. So the strangely bent Monterey pines
of the Del Monte Forest will forever be heart disturbing in a love
lost minor key.

That black night, as I stepped out into the Cantina's parking
lot, a cool breeze blew in from the ocean, carrying with it a scent
that confirmed that freshly lost love was the dearest thing that had
ever existed in my life.

I stood there frozen. Poised before my car, keys in hand. It was so quiet. Dead still and almost no lights, just the night sky, the new moon and in that darkness the Carmel Valley became the farthest most outlying remotest shitfuck patch of Earth imaginable.

Here I was, back on the Monterey Peninsula and it's happened again. Alone. And . . . She was with another guy. At that very moment. I just knew it. It made me shiver.

AIYEEEH!! AIYEEEH!! AIYEEEH!! AIYEEEH!!

The beast stomped across the tranquil Carmel Valley, tearing shit apart all over the place, its red eyes blazing into the heart of me.

AIYEEEH!! AIYEEEH!! AIYEEEH!! AIYEEEH!!

I drove back into Monterey with a timid dream of finding some sort of gala nightlife section of town where people were gathered with drinks in hand and laughter and gaiety filled the air. Music and babes aplenty will spill out onto the sidewalk and my wounds will be balmed. I will move to Monterey and lead a life filled with more friends and sex than ever before.

I drove past Fisherman's Wharf, lost now in the thin tendrils of fog and the vampire visions of lost love.

As I headed downtown, Monterey had the look of a city recently smote down with a highly contagious and deadly disease. Doors were bolted shut at 8 P.M. on a Tuesday. Not a soul roamed the streets except for a few stray cats that scurried off in the face of my car's headlights. They were rather mangy and appeared to be coughing.

There *were* no loud voices and neon signs guiding me to the Gatsbian Period of my life. The one in which I dress smartly in fine suits, drink fine cocktails or sip Highland single malts or XOs wrung from grand cru vines tended by ancient French vintners.

Oh, the wit. The laughter. It's so fucking fun and sophisticated that I can hardly stand it. My life becomes the very definition of what is cool in the industrialized world.

And the girls, well, I don't have to tell you about the girls, I say noddingly a nudge nudge wink wink in me voice. Those silk evening gowns with the spaghetti arm straps that keep slipping off their milky soft shoulders are all you need to know.

But such is not the case in Monterey that night. I instead find myself in a town instantly and permanently lethal to one's single life. A four-block walking tour of downtown Monterey convinced me that I would never again have sex if I remained within its city limits.

So I decided to head back home. To Berkeley. Back home, but not before a drive-by. I had a drive-by to commit on Ramona Avenue where I had once shared the one and only apartment I ever lived in with the First One.

I drove the quiet flat square gridded streets with amazing clarity. I knew just where I was going more than ten years after the fact.

I turned down the street and turned off the radio (they weren't playing the proper breakup period song right then) and slowed down 'til I was nearly stopped as I came upon the apartment where we used to live. Somehow, I've ended up, more than ten years later, on the same street, looking at that old apartment, in the same sort of predicament with another woman.

I remembered riding home each night from the crêpery on my bike, up and over the hill between Monterey and Carmel. You could always count on the barking of the sea lions each and every night.

Urf! Urf! Urf!

Off in the dark and the distance the sea lions comforted me almost more than her back then. She was sweet as could be and her love and nurture and devotion far beyond anything my first girl mentality could conceive.

It came out of nowhere (well, looking back I guess it didn't *exactly* come out of nowhere). Rather, same as with K——, it came after nine months of growing dissatisfaction on my part where I told her of my deep dark doubts as to the viability of our relationship. After about two hundred days of that, it came out of nowhere.

I can remember it as clear as day. It was right after the '84 Games in L.A. Never let your woman go unchaperoned to an Olympics Field Hockey semifinals. You can't trust men who go to field hockey games—they're sharks. Anyway, she came back from the Games and announced to me that she had met someone else. We were living together at the time and her announcement was impossible to fathom. It was so out of character for her. She was such a quiet shy little blonde it was as though she had announced that she was once a man or worked for Oliver North on the covert shipping of arms to Nicaragua.

But there it was.

Kee-Rack!!

She had not only *met* someone else, but she had fallen in *love* during Pakistan's dramatic second-half comeback over Holland. She was in love, she was moving out, there was talk of marriage. Of course I tried to reason with her (remember, I was in the midst of my months-long process of deciding whether or not to leave her. You can't get fired when you're contemplating quitting. That's the worst possible time to get fired!), but it was useless and thus began my lifelong streak of never, ever, fucking never! reconciling with a single woman I've ever dated. Every one of my relationships has been like milk. When the time's up, when they go bad, they're bad. That's it. There's no repair work in store.

I'd head into work, to Perkins' Crêpery, in a dazed state, stunned and so very alone, fully convinced that I would never ever hold a woman in my arms again (while trying to convince Mr. Perkins that, no, I really don't think putting canned tuna in the lemon Jell-

O is any sort of cutting edge culinary statement), certain that my cock's career had been cut tragically short.

One weekend, the last before I moved out, I decided to take a walk while let's call her Arlene carefully applied makeup for her big date tonight—Don't bother staying up. I'm not sure how late I'll get back . . . if I even do. See, she still cares for me and doesn't want me to wait up for her. Damn her soul.

It was gray out and a light mist fell, a very fine mist that brought the gray down all around me, deep into my brain. It seemed bone-chilling. I was practically shivering from it all.

I don't know that I ever felt so alone as that late afternoon, walking the dead suburban streets of Monterey, my nose to the ground, occasionally looking upward as if to question why God (who I only chatted with at times of extreme duress or to blame for shit) had done me so wrong.

I continued on for a while. No one was out on the streets. No children played outside, hardly a car slipped by, the only sound the wind through the huge eucalyptus and pine. There was nothing until I heard a voice. Someone called out to me and I wasn't listening the first time. I looked up and there was a young man standing on the porch. He called to me again.

"Are you . . . ?"

"What?" I asked. I didn't get the last part.

"Are you Ray?" he repeated.

"Am I Ray?" I asked.

"No, not Ray." He now cupped his hands around his mouth to get his urgent message across. "I *said*, 'Are you gay?' "

I heard that. "No," I answered angrily (not that there's anything wrong . . .). "I'm not gay."

Oh great, a special new friend reaches out to me, I thought as I crumpled ever so slightly even farther into the pavement and continued on my way. He's hoping for some easy lovin' without even having to leave his porch. He's hoping I'll just say, Sure, I'm gay as shit. Let me come on over, suck you off and then I'll be on my way.

Or maybe he could somehow sense my vulnerability. Maybe he could tell from the vantage point of his Sunday afternoon porch that I had just been fired from my steady job at Heterosexuality 'N' Stuff and he only wanted to tell me of the positions open at Butts 'N' Things.

But I wasn't about to go gay. At least not right off (as I looped back around to the what I scarily imagined was the now empty apartment I promised myself to give dating a twelve-month try and then at least *consider* celibacy before taking the plunge). I was about to step into a new phase of my life. A Brave New World of confusion, rejection and sweet success. The nonvirgin World of Dating that somehow took me to this same street staring lost in thought at an apartment I once lived in with the first one. The first woman who it didn't work out with.

What's with that? I don't know but as I drove back to Berkeley this Monterey radio station had the greatest blues program on and this made me happy.

But really, I wasn't even there. I wasn't even really driving home from Monterey listening to T-Bone Walker, lost in my thoughts of two of the four women I've ever loved. I was in reality sitting in a chair watching rain run down a black window.

e-mail

Subject:
  Babeeocchh!
Date:
  Tues, 16, Dec 1997 15:52:29 +0100
From:
  MacElvie@antik-fryc.cz

I have been going to these balls, formal dances, you know, and having an interesting time. I shagged mi chica outside during one last Friday, and then she had to go home at two. I stayed and took another girl home, which was kind of stupid because I had told my girlfriend to come over at eleven in the morning, and I didn't go to sleep until five, with this other girl. Thank the fucking lord above that I heard my alarm clock at nine and got up, made some coffee, and as slyly as possible told this girl I had to go to Prague, which required me to go with her into town, act like I was going to the bus station, and haul ass back to my pad (these trips involved two trams and two buses) only minutes before chica arrived. The ball had been the ball of the school where I teach and chica attends. Luckily, this girl,who was good to go, was not a student there. So far, nothing has come of the situation with the chica in the little school library. She has started seeing some guy who goes to the school and seems just as interested in not talking to anybody about it as I am. Plus, I think she knows I'm seeing the other girl. My luck is going good, but it is probably running thin, and I have the overwhelming feeling the shit will hit the fan soon enough. Until then, however, fuck it. I am having fun.

Well, man, gotta hit it. Late, M

north county girl, date #13

The hot little NC Girl dropped by tonight. She was wearing these painted-on tight jeans and a tight stretchy blouse revealing all her juicy curves in all the right places on her small full body.

We sat on the couch. Another woman on the couch who won't go, but they sit on the couch and let me fool around a bit, slip in a kiss now and again and the North County Girl even had a little something in her kisses this time. Oh to fuck her! I thought as I ran my hands along her body, around her tight round ass, along her fine thighs packed into that sky blue denim. I could see the white lace of her bra under the packed blouse holding up those hefty handfuls of breast she has. Arrghh!!

She invited me over for Thursday. I say yes. I can't help but fall for it, except this time I'm not so easily pushed around. I tell her to come over to my place instead. If nothing else I should at least get to be lazy about it. As far as I'm concerned, I've been putting out far too much effort for far too little in return.

Come Thursday will be the record-setting (and with each successive date the record grows) fourteenth date without sex or even any genital exploration. Secondary sexual characteristics represent the limit. I lost my virginity to a virgin by the tenth date. That had once been the standard and now, almost twenty years later, I'm having even more trouble. I'll head into Thursday evening like some sort of anti–Cal Ripken, always ready to report, never miss a game, they just never put me in.

But I continue to walk my world with the hopes that someday some girl will allow me to fuck her. That there exists an actual living breathing woman who is interested in my genitalia and all the tricks it can supposedly perform.

It had me thinking about Chance and Fate and Destiny and many of the possible explanations we might tack on to explain my sudden slump. One has to be careful with that sort of soul-searching (and I wonder what it means that most of my soul-searching revolves around my dick). If I take to wearing blue socks for luck I can no longer call myself an Existentialist and tossing the Ching means I spit in a Christian god's face. But ultimately I'm a nonsectarian opportunist and a lazy one at that, which is really the benchmark for any opportunist worth his salt. I'll pick up virtually any sort of philosophy or half-baked Way of Life (as long as it comes from the classics section. I'm not too keen on the self-help section or the words of TV philosophers who appear on *Oprah*) short of Deepak Chopra. I just don't trust that Hindi snake oil salesman, not to mention it was one of two books in the entire house of Nurse! That can't be a good sign, Deepak and *The Stand* by Stephen King. How much of a philosopher can he really be if she fell for him?

aiyeeeh!! aiyeeeh!!

... She had called the week before and arranged to stop by and pick up a couple of things ... she left behind on her midnight escape that was our breakup. I had a slowly shrinking pile of her boxes, a lamp, some sort of indoor exercise thing. I was the "storage locker," we'd joke over the phone. It was what made me a nice guy (instead of the Scoundrel I wanted to be), keeping her stuff in my place, not burning it or dumping it all over her desk at work one afternoon.

Karen, okay? That's her fucking name. Let me say it again. Karen, all right?! And five years, that's how long we were together. Five fucking years. Okay?

That was the hardest part to take. The sheer length of it. If it's not going to work out let's be done with it in two years tops. Two weeks, three months, a year and a half or forever. These are the proper lengths for relationships.

And today she's coming over to pick up some things.

AIYEEEH!! AIYEEEH!!

It breaches! But I come equipped today. I break out the artillery, I've got Raymond Burr taking careful readings. Today we will beat back the beast. Take that and that! My rationalizations (she didn't read, we liked different music, no threesomes or anal sex) momentarily subdues the monster but Karen is a worthy opponent and counters with laser-accurate activations of my memories of "us" in happy poignant moments (the snow up at Monitor Pass, that Christmas with my family when she was my home, not them). But I answer back with bitter accusations of her doing me wrong; I've got her in retreat and worked myself up into a bit of a lather, but I remember the women since she's been gone and then I hear the footsteps coming up the stairs and I almost feel sick.

brioche

I walked out to her car with her. With Karen. Still carin' about
Karen; it can make me sick. Sick with love? I don't fucking know.
I mostly feel the warm and squishy stuff when she's not around,
but today, in broad daylight, with her by my side (we even walked
down to the store like we did a million times so long ago), I can't
deny it all. I can't pretend it's all just water long ago under the
bridge, that it never hurts ever.

And maybe neither can she 'cause she got sad once when she saw
the cat that used to be hers and she cried for a second and made
that sad woman's face that finally relieves me of all my bile and
floods me instead with tenderness. When I wish I might make it
better for her for once rather than the other way around.

She wiped her eyes with her sleeve and blew her nose with a
wadded-up Kleenex and looked at me sadly for a moment. Neither
of us said a word. Not a fucking thing.

I don't know, maybe it was the cat. I don't know.

Either way, as we walk out to her car it seems entirely possible
that you can be sad and forever-lost-love in love with someone you
can't be with. They drive away and somehow this over-now, once-
great love affair driving off down the street becomes a heartbreaking
unattainable ideal/curse. That's how it felt when I began to head

back to the house. It felt bad, but it also felt good in a way, too, these golden days looked back upon.

At my door I abruptly turned around and headed to the bakery. The brioche. I simply had to exorcise it. It was the final demon embedded still in my brain that was preventing the great blossoming that I know was struggling to get out. I marched down to the bakery that created the damn brioches morning in and morning out for the past 322 days. They paid no heed at all to my personal brioche trauma, continuing in their relentless production of said brioche, neither observing a moratorium nor slowing production. They made not even the slightest effort in regards to the sad heartbreak the brioche had come to be.

I didn't even eat the fucking things until Karen came along! I was happy with my scone or baguette chunk. Sure, I'd delved into their misshapen strangely named chocolate things, but I was a scone man and happy about it too—but no, not her. No, those brioches caught her eye the very first time she stepped in. I was squiring her around my neighborhood in the morning after she'd spent the night. I wanted her to try the scones. I'd been talking them up.

"Ooh, those look good." Her eyes lit up as she was drawn to the bin of brioches, wrapped up like a ball of yarn, wrapped round like a Oaxacan cheese ball, studded with raisins and glistening with sugar and a baked egg wash. She reached for a plump one.

It was brioche from there on out and they were good with a cup of coffee sitting in the jungling spring green growth in my unkempt but beautiful backyard. I forsook my scone. I abandoned my scone swayed by her love of the brioche.

But the day came, right after she left, when I ran back like a little baby to my original love. I cleaved myself to my scone like a desperate born-again. I would buy my morning scone while trying to sadly avoid seeing the binful of brioche which had come to mean this mythical "Us" that hadn't existed for the last two years "we" were together but which sprang up bigger than life when she left. The brioche expanded into a sad symbol, a breakfast baked good option that overgrew any decent limits. It came to represent far more than any eight-ounce baked good should.

But a new day has arrived . . . I think. The reign is over. I'm taking a stand.

As I step inside the store Time slips again and I don't know to where now, but to somewhere else, for the bakery feels different this morning. Her special conclusion "This place really is a dump" keeps ringing in my ear.

I walk straight toward the bin. Yes, a brioche. That's what I want. I really do love the sweet cinnamon texture and occasional raisin reward hidden within its folds.

I take a big yeasty bite out of it. It's the finest brioche. I can see that now. That's where Time has sent me today, to a land where a brioche is just a brioche and potstickers are just potstickers and . . . She is not Karen but some Phantom Limb of Love. Long ago amputated but still wired into my brain so that it itches now and again when I'm alone or feel lonely or late at night when the weight of the darkness weighs down upon my spirit, but really there's nothing there. I reach to scratch the itch and that's where I get lost because it's no longer there.

the sad cafe

Christmas was coming and the rains kept coming and coming and just wouldn't stop all December long and one day Marco even said to me, "We're gonna be all washed up if business doesn't get any better," without thinking of the irony of it and soon the crews were reduced to skeleton levels.

Marco was too nice to let anyone go but our hours kept getting cut back more and more. We were down to just above the labor force that operates your typical hot dog stand. A waiter, cook, dishwasher and Marco who when it was slow enough either sent the waitress home or let her stay and cover the tables while he worked a special Marco shift that consisted of extreme worrying, actual hand-wringing above the cash register and hypnotic staring downs of the front door. The few diners that came in were quizzed seriously by Marco as to what was wrong with business.

Toward the end of another desperately slow night (even weekends were beginning to dry up) I stepped out back to get some supplies from the dry storage and saw a man standing just outside the door in the shadows. He scared the shit out of me for a moment until I saw his timidity. It was a street person. He had that ruddy even in winter complexion of a man always out of doors, the stiff matted hair, the shabby clothes, the exploding tennies.

He seemed to have something on his mind but he didn't say a word, he just stared at me, stared right through me. He stared at me with those street eyes, eyes that aren't all there, eyes that spend much of their time viewing the private worlds of their mind.

"What's up, man?" I asked him. "You lookin' for something?"

He seemed skittish and scared like the mutts that sometimes circled the back Dumpster in the hopes of scraps of meat.

"You got anything here?" he finally asked. "Anything left over? . . . It's for my dog."

It was against rules to give out food to the homeless. It's not that Marco and Gina were so coldhearted, it's just that you couldn't get a name out on the streets. There were too many of them and you'd end up with an army of them showing up every night looking for a handout from a place practically going out of business.

"I don't know . . . we're not supposed to," I said.

He just looked at me, embarrassed, resigned and defeated. "It's for my dog. . . ."

It was killing me him pretending to have a dog. Like I'd be more likely to help his fictional dog than help him. "Look, I got some bread. How 'bout some bread?"

He didn't say a word and I shrugged.

"Okay." He nodded. "That'd be all right."

I looked over to the trash can, where I'd just thrown out some bread scraps. I considered them for a second. I really did. My natural capitalist commandments told me, *Thou shalt work for thine bread,* but I just couldn't do it. Here he was, down on his luck in those beat-up shoes and it's gonna be cold tonight and maybe it'll pour again and he's just got that thin ratty coat. I went back into the kitchen and quickly threw together a Parma ham sandwich, the sandwich which had comforted me this long El Niño winter.

As I carefully pulled the slices of ham from the wax paper, I realized how much that sandwich had meant to me. How it had sustained me over the months. It had restored me, as is the mission of a restaurant. To restore with its fare and there I'd be five days a week at the table slicing up and assembling these great sandwiches for the masses that had failed to materialize at Marco's Trattoria—but I did have one more up my sleeve: my finest example of the Parma ham sandwich (use only the finest of fine slices of prosciutto. I'd determined the proper thickness to the micron. The proper layering of the ham. The bread toasted up just so, the exact number of Parmesan shaves). I kept looking over my shoulder hoping Gina or Marco wouldn't come back into the kitchen.

I placed it into the hand of this ruddy roughed-up street character. "Here you go."

He took it and looked at it suspiciously for a second as it sat in his hand. "Is there any meat?"

He couldn't see the meat. You don't put that much on it. I'm telling you, I'd worked out the exact amount of ham (and exact thickness of this ham) and cheese over the course of the novel.

It was the way he asked it. Not like some of the rude and pretentious diners. He asked innocently, childlike.

"There's some nice ham," I assured him.

He smiled nervously and turned to walk away and then looked back. "Uh, thanks, man."

I turned around and Gina was standing there. I could tell she'd seen the entire thing and I felt hot from my red hands.

"You think I'm some bitch, don't you?" she accused me.

She said it with such vehemence that it caught me doubly off guard. I had, more than once, thought and even said to Niko "What a bitch" 'cause it was true she was nasty at times.

"You think since I won't give the beggars food I'm some heartless bitch."

"No I don't."

"You don't understand." She looked at me and her anger verged on sadness, her fists clenched and neck tensed. "There's just too many. I can't even take care of Marco and me and here you are so very generous, giving away things that aren't yours."

"I'm sorry . . . ," I began, but she'd turned on her heel and walked away and I felt like a creep.

After work I decided to go to the pub across the street and end my ten-year experiment in sitting silently alone on a bar stool and strike up a conversation. With a man, thus nearly ensuring success. I'll mention the game. It'll be a piece of cake.

sweet surrender or capitulation?

Hallelujah!! There is some sort of justice in the world for how else to explain that I find myself after so very long back in the pussy saddle once again? I could not even admit to myself how long it had been since I'd been inside, so to speak. It had been so very very long. Not counting the anomalous Jane (or the ultra-anomalous Freak), it had been sometime from mid-June to December 17, a day that will forever live in ecstasy.

The girl with the record-setting number of dates has ended her own record. I'm still not sure it's really her but maybe some hot, dark-haired horny twin sister she's never told me about (Marcy, the identical twin temptress who cares for nothing but unbridled lust, as opposed to Darcy, her virginal counterpart who longs for the days when marriage came *before* oral sex, not after).

But who am I to question the workings of the mysterious El Niño-addled cosmos? Who am I but a mere mortal man allowed at long last to delve into her sopping-wet goodies? Her panties are practically drenched she's made us wait so long. Did I finally wear her down? Has her mind changed? Has she allowed lust to carry the moment? Is it The Holidays?

I don't know for I've not changed. I haven't become younger or richer or grown more hair or muscles or increased my wit or compassion levels. It's all remained the same except now, *Whoop, there it is!*

She wants it and I give it to her and I can see she's actually really enjoying it and we're going at it hot and heavy with twisted sheets round our ankles and sweat on my forehead. Her full breasts spill out of that fantastic fine black bra and her kisses are almost frantic as though it had been me making us wait all these weeks and I slip on the jimmy and slip in like I was meant to be inside all along, slide it deeply into her tight wet pussy, my hands gripping her slim hips firmly, her full breasts bouncing with each thrust, a grimace of pleasure on her face as she grabs the back of my neck and calls out my name. She grips my arms with both hands for dear life on her back in that tall soft bed and when I'm giving it to her hard (my cock some miracle invention, its permanent hardness rooted to my very core) she seems to like it best of all, when she moans and groans hardest of all.

It's what I've been waiting for all this time. I've been dying for her wet warm capture, her soft round ass, the erotic heft of her breasts when she climbs on top, the delicious view as she positions herself to be taken from behind.

And then, with the candle flickering in the afterglow, the funk-fresh musk of her little beast sheets, the smell of excitement and pussy on her breath, she falls immediately asleep right there in my arms as my mind begins to spin as it always will in the bed of a new one.

We woke up and luckily it was a workday because I always have to flee the scene like some petty burglar. She was sweet as can be and the dawn brought no new morning uncomfortableness (perhaps there's a method to her madness). We even went at it again; she was sopping and gasping again and came as I went down on her, luxuriating in her salty sweet juices while she dug away at her swollen clit with her middle finger.

The goodies have been taken and it's time to run. I have work as a cover and she makes me the finest cup of Turkish coffee wearing a thin nightgown under a dark blue silk robe. Barefoot, her calves look marvelous when she reaches up into the cupboard to fetch a cup and with one more kiss she asks, "When will I see you again?"

Soon, I thought, for I was hot on her and as I drove off the coffee began to hit me and with the motion of the car as it got up to freeway speed so too did my spirit accelerate and my life got up to a true man's speed and all was right. I sipped my coffee and could smell her on my hand and face (she asked if I wanted to take a shower but I wanted to save that smell; it's a valuable thing. Her amazing aroma is a thing men just don't have).

Then after work I called her up and I came over, and whereas before, before the consummation, before on all those other dates, when making dinner or talking or going to a movie or for a walk all held promise, hope and tension over the prospect of sex, now that's all I wanted to get to. Now, the making of the dinner and the watching of the movie were endless to sit through, but I had that vague dread I sometimes get when I first hook up with a girl, the body/psyche's first hint of allergic reaction. The foreign body that's invaded physically and emotionally. My God what have I done? What does this all mean?

There's always some sort of allergic reaction. Only our own bodies are for ourselves. The question was how much of an allergic reaction was coming and would it be a swift disease that kills in a matter of weeks or one of those slow fever type ones that take a full season to pass or maybe one of those that settle into a comfy groove where your body takes to the dose, where the girl becomes the cure and life is now grand.

And grand it was after work on a Saturday night. She felt perfect-sized in my arms under the covers, lying on her side, her back to my front. I run my hand along her soft skin. It's an amazement, the skin of women, far more miraculous than my own. I run my hand the length of her, from her shoulders, down her arm, along her waist that dips in slightly, along the immediate erotic curve of her hips, down her small thighs as far as I can reach and I'm pleased. I'm so pleased by her size and shape that I put my arm around her waist and pull her toward me and she likes this and with a grand smile on my face we slip into a long winter's nap.

children of the delta

The very next week I was somehow roped into driving to the dreary flat falsely boundless Delta with the North County Girl, my hands gripping the steering wheel feeling I'd been tricked, constantly asking childlike, "Are we there yet?"

The night before it was the phone ringing, her sweet voice asking in an actual eager tone I found impossibly irresistible and me within minutes in the car turning over the engine and over the bridge and it's late at night, but she wants me there. Miss Reluctant is calling suddenly and I don't mind in the very least. I can't wait for under the sheets and the thick comforter. She had two and they cooked me at night, but she promised to take one off 'cause she wants me there.

I drive over the back bridge, the long humpbacked Richmond-San Rafael Bridge eager as can be. It's late at night but I'm willing, no question, and it'll be straight to bed. As I accelerate after paying the toll I'm thinking of her wonderful smile, the great warmth and aroma that rises off her neck at night as she sleeps. The night is brilliant clear, you can see it all from the Richmond-San Rafael: the Gate, the City, the lights, the Bay. It's cold out. I'm heading to a warm woman's bed. Life is perfect.

●　　●　　●

I spent yet another night snuggled against her warm form, as another front had come ashore late that night. It woke me up, (she was peacefully asleep), and I listened to the rains pound outside like I was the cat that got the mouse.

She had mentioned something in passing as I fell asleep about a get-together at her sister's the next day and I was invited which made me, wrongly it turned out, assume that the choice was up to me. While no arms were twisted after another enthusiastic session of morning sex followed up by another flawless cup of coffee (this woman could whip out the greatest cup of coffee; she didn't even drink the stuff but her technique was unapproachable and her range stunning: authentic three-times-to-the-boil Turkish, French-press wizardry in a plunging-neckline robe while I groped—her breasts, once strictly off limits, are now my toys and mine alone—basic Melitta hand-poured drip filters. She could cajole a fine cup of Joe out of a vintage Mr. Coffee that was in just-out-of-the-box condition).

I couldn't say no. It is an unwritten rule. Within the hour after having hot sex most requests have to be granted: shopping, flea market visits, her parading you past some close female friend, or even the dreaded relatives (though that was pushing it at such an early stage, in my opinion).

But I almost thought I was in love and without a care after the first few sips of an amazing cafe au lait of French-pressed aged Sumatra.

Until the get-together. Now I don't know if we can see each other anymore. It wasn't even the amazing suburban home unit set in the floodplains of the Delta fifty miles east of the Gate. One of those hermetically sealed Xenophobia Pointe community affairs protected from the outside strange. It was all that questionless suburban breeding that's easy for those not of the suburban breeder mind-set to forget.

Kids.

"I want to have a family someday," she said enthusiastically as I tightened the grip on the steering wheel. "Don't you?"

"Ummm, kids are nice. I love their enthusiasm." Good one, I thought.

"We could have one or two. I think that'd be about right."

We? I think as I wring molten plastic out of the steering wheel. Oh . . . my . . . God. What have I gotten into?

"I want a girl," she smiled, and stroked my forearm.

"Heh," I sort of smile-laughed. "Isn't anything good on the radio?" Luckily Foreigner had come to the rescue and I now concentrated on finding a good song.

The first thing that hit me when the introductions were made before the spread of suburban hors d'oeuvres in the downstairs rec room with pool table and a wall filled with guns (he was a hunter, which I kinda liked) was that inside these hermetically sealed environs with the kitchen so clean and the walls so big and bare and the furniture so perfect, they were breeding. At an alarming rate!

The place was crawling with toddlers. There were only three other women besides the North County Girl and yet six toddlers under the age of four crawled and climbed about, while one woman swole with child spoke with a second woman who said "We're planning for another. Just not sure when yet."

They were planning. They're all planning. I looked at the Girl from the North County. She's got a plan.

I had one now, too. Especially after her best friend's husband came up to me and looked at all the kids terrorizing about and shook his head. "All these kids. My wife's really putting on the pressure. She wants two." My plan was to never again even consider the nonuse of a condom.

The talk revolved around the kids, their jobs, home buying, weddings and how the women make it all work out with the day care and the preschool yadda-yadda-yadda. I quickly gathered that the children were a collection of the finest examples of what Mankind (and his seed) had to offer. They were the sweetest and most special and amazing and miraculous and charming collection of future Nobel Prize—winning doctors, entrepreneurs, beautiful women and famous athletes ever assembled before a buffet of jalapeño poppers, spinach dip, those all-the-same-size tiny carrots that come in bags, an actual red holiday minced-nut-covered cheese ball, Cook's sparkling wine and a small refrigerator packed with cans of Budweiser.

The amazingly large future football player (I mistook the four-year-old for a lad of six with retarded social skills. At one point the budding bully broke out a pair of nun-chuks and began brandishing them violently, but the parents didn't seem to mind so who am I to wonder?) seemed sullen and reveled in the pushing over backwards of the coverall-clad drooling snot-nosed nineteen-monther who refused to be deterred. The tiny toddler would not be put in his place by the four-year-old bully. I liked that. The nineteen-monther was pretty cool.

As we drove home the NC Girl snuggled next to me and said as happy as a clam, "Weren't the kids *so* cute?"

"Mmmm; yeah . . . ," I somehow said.

"This is so romantic." She looked up at me and smiled sweetly. Gulp.

takin' care of the seed

The very next day I told Niko about the party, about the NC Girl and the scary bully child, and wondered aloud whether or not that many kids birthed by three women wasn't out of line, and as soon as I finished she said,

"Three women, six kids? No, that ain't nothing. Did I ever tell you about my niece, the sixteen-year old? Remember her?"

"Yeah, Niko, I remember, but I don't have time for her right now. I got my own problems, I think."

"Yeah you do."

"Huh?"

"You better be takin' care of that semen."

"What?!"

"That's right."

"Whaddaya mean I got problems?"

"Control the seed, ma brotha. . . ."

"My seed?!?"

"Yeah, dispose of your semen. Take . . . control . . . of the se-men."

"I'm using a condom."

Niko looked at me like you poor naive little man. "How long do you stay after sex?" Niko was mathematical-serious now.

220

"What?"

"You there for a few hours? Or is it Bang! I'm outta there? Gimme a sandwich and I'm gone?"

"Not always. Sometimes I'm there the night."

"Mmm-hmmmm," she hummed deep and thick with that scary voodoo warning of hers. Niko could scare the shit out of me more than anyone. "Condom, I hope? Or do I even have to ask?"

"Yeah, condom. I told you condom!" I'm burning over that one time we didn't. "I even throw 'em in the wastebasket, too."

"The wastebasket!?" she practically mocked me.

"What's wrong with the wastebasket?"

"What, and have her draining that thing? An' next thing you know comin' up pregnant?"

"Come on, you think she's taking my semen from disposed condoms she's fished out of the wastebasket after I leave?" I got a hot flash around my neck.

"I have this friend, Glenda, and she . . ."

I'd heard all about Glenda. Glenda was some sort of Loch Ness Monster of Fertility friend of Niko's. I mean, she'd be getting pregnant making out on a couch, pants never pulled down, or while on women-only camping trips.

"You think she's tappin' my load after I'm gone? Artificially inseminating . . ."

"Just check your shit, Carl. Keep control of the seed is all I'm sayin'."

"Mmmm," I replied, unnerved by the twin images of the NC Girl's overgrown nun-chuk weilding nephew and that Lifestyles Ultrasensitive sitting in her bedside wastebasket, carrying millions of possibly still-viable seed.

e-mail

Subject:
  Cool Moe D
Date:
  Mon, 22 Dec 1997 16:52:38 +0100
From:
  macilvie@antik-fryc.cz

So, dude. Glad to hear about you being back in the pussy saddle. Investments always suck, but in the end, sometimes they're worth it. Actually, I don't believe that shit, but its sounds nice. Work that ass all you can. Then crumple it and throw it away. When the relationship analysis comes up, lie. "Sure, baby, you know I love you, wanna be with you forever. Its all about cooperation, working together, sharing our lives. Now SUCK MY MUTHERFUCKING DICK!"

It works for me, especially when the girl don't speak ze English. Anyways, I have been actually sticking it to just one lately. I think I told you about her. Little blondie, just seventeen, and she's a 20 something seventeen. Which means, in this country, when she turns 26, she'll be looking like a Babushka. But, now, the body on that babe. NEVER! in my life after I leave this country will I have an opportunity to wet my beak as I have here. The sheer joy.

But let me tell you, boy, Hungarians are quite the shizznit. They got that olive skin you crave so much. Budapest was a fucking good time. Great wine, great food, great women. But I didn't get to fuck any of them. The closest I came was actually to this American chick, which really gave me a big heapin' dose of exactly what I don't like about American chicks. This girl, also to my disappointment, was a little too much like Rita. A little in appearance, but mainly in attitude, that oversensitive, "I just read a book on feminism" attitude which just really makes me want to say sexist things while I stick my dick in her ear kind of thing.

When am I coming back? Not sure, but . . . I don't know. I'm beginning to think I might never leave, especially if I can get a sweet job, and something other than teaching. I like it and all, but . . .

Well, man, gotta hit it.

Late,
HRD M

maxie

The next day I go to work happy that someone, especially since it's my buddy, can be a true scoundrel.

At one point as I walk back from the dry storage I see this guy at the counter and Gina leaning in a little too close. He was about my age and I slowed for the smallest fraction of a second, just enough for her to look up and see me see them. I looked away and sped back up like nothing happened and she straightened up and made some comments about a reservation like nothing's happened, but I'm pretty certain both of us know something happened, that entire personal universes teetered on the brink.

Back in the kitchen, while pounding out some veal for some old-school veal parmigiana, my mind burned with the scandal of it all. Was Gina having an affair? Jesus-fucking-Christ is nothing sacred? Is everybody even more scoundrelish than I dreamed of being? What the fuck is going on?

Gina came back into the kitchen and shot me a quick look that was a combination of warning and fear that confirmed my suspicions as to what was going on.

We worked together that night, her on sauté, me on grill, silently, same way Rock'n'Rollero and I do, and it was weird. My feelings were hurt in some odd way. It overwhelmed my surprise even. That she'd sleep with someone else was bad enough, but I felt as betrayed as I imagined poor Marco would feel if he knew. I mean, if there was going to be any fooling around I thought it would be with me 'cause only we understood. Only Gina and I really cared about the food. Only Gina was serious about food like me. That's when I liked her the most. That's when her dark brow and black eyes drew me in the most. When she became fierce and loving and absorbed in the food.

She left early because it was so slow and that night Maxie and I hung out after work out back.

We were sitting out there in the dark behind the restaurant, Maxie and me, sitting on stacks of plastic milk crates. It was cold outside, but dry for once and because of all the rains the air was fresh as a hundred years ago and a cool welcome after the heat and sweat of the kitchen.

Maxie was smoking a cigarette and we were both sipping our shift beer. He reached far under one of the wooden pallets piled high with flattened cardboard boxes and wooden produce crates waiting to be recycled.

"¿Donde está, amigo? Ahh, aqui, hah-ha, aqui compañero."

His hand reappeared from beneath the pile bearing a bottle of Sauza Conmemorativo: his hidden stash. It glistened golden and brown in a stray remnant of light coming from the kitchen's back door. I handed Maxie a piece of lime.

"Está listo, amigo?"

I nodded and Max unscrewed the top and took a long tug off the bottle. He exhaled as he handed me the bottle and calmly sucked on a wedge of lime.

I took a deep breath and brought the bottle to my lips. After a hot near-sour mouthful I sucked on the lime.

"Bueno, compañero. Uno más."

"No, uno más para ti." I handed him the bottle.

Maxie took another good slug and then a drag off his cigarette. "Uno más."

"Okay," I said, and took another shot. My face felt flush and my stomach went hot and slightly sour. I looked back toward the kitchen. It was making those warm comforting humming and clanking sounds. I could hear Marco's animated voice as he held court at the Table. A narrow band of yellow light spilled out the door and onto the driveway, not quite reaching where we sat in the darkness.

I set the bottle down. I now felt warm and comfortable. I looked up in the sky, where hung a tiny onion sliver of frigid silver moon and a few stars refusing to be washed out by the city's lights.

Maxie began to tell me of his land, his hometown just south of Veracruz. Boca del Río. It has simply the best seafood, en el todo mundo, he told me with great pride. In Boca del Río they had two kinds of shrimp, freshwater and Gulf. Maxie was emphatic about there being two kinds.

"Dos!" He held up two fingers. The local women would bring them up to Veracruz by second-class bus and sell them in the zocalo with limes and chilied salt. They were highly prized.

"¿Con una cerveza?! Ah." Max smiled and reached into his pocket for another cigarette.

It sounded so wonderful. The shrimp, the big-armed women carrying them through the zocalo. He said I could stay with his family there. I was already gone. Now that I had a girl I often wanted to escape.

Max pulled out a Marlboro from his dishwasher's shirt and lit a match. It sizzled to life and lit his face as he cupped his hand around the cigarette. All the timeworn creases in Maxie's face came to life in the flickering sodium yellow light of the match.

He was a great Master of Life in my opinion that night and on many other nights. He questioned very little and enjoyed all that might come his way and as he tossed the match into the night and extinction I wanted to be just like Maxie and live life in some lively manner on the Gulf of Mexico.

But the moment the match went black the wave passed and I wasn't at Maxie's family's in Boca del Río, but sitting on a flattened cardboard box on an empty upturned milk crate, and that homeless guy, he's got exploded tennis shoes on his feet in the dead of winter and Gina's cheating on Marco and I'm not in Veracruz *or* Prague and then I thought of the North County Girl one more time because she's a natural comfort even when I'm trying to escape her. She's turning into the girl I *should* be in love with and while this might normally be all quite troubling I'm sitting with Maxie in the dark in this perfect wonderful moment and we're not saying a word and I feel at peace with myself and the cosmos for once.

christmas

So, let me begin to relate it all to you. Marco's was closed. There was no work and in a gesture of generosity beyond their means Christmas was a paid day off. I began mine at the crack of dawn nearly because my presence was required at my aunt and uncle's house at 8:15 for the traditional Christmas breakfast featuring much pork and much pastry.

We're out in Vallejo and after a few cups of coffee and a big sweet roll we all hop in the car and head to some technical cousin's (though not by blood) where this year's feasting begins. The day was brilliantly clear, the light an amazing golden with a hint of cold in the rushes of wind that whipped up the streets, past all the same houses and the many children out riding bikes shiny, bright and new.

As we stepped into the house I could smell the bacon and sausages a-sizzlin'. These people loved their morning pork products and even had the empty coffee can set up for the quarts of rendered bacon, sausage and ham fat that was a daily part of their lives. They were pros and my ancestral heart revved throatily in anticipation of the feast.

Love of pork (not to mention pastries) showed on my family. The women were for the most part simply massive. The kind where walking entails a swinging of the arms and general torso to facilitate forward motion. The men had the classic I'm-mostly-lean-except-for-this-medicine-ball-I-have-tucked-under-my-T-shirt look.

To show I was down with the Ds, one of the family, I dove into the stack of crispy mahogany bacon and cut my fork through many a sweating little Jimmy Dean's sausage I'd plucked cooling on a fat-soaked paper towel. And you better recognize! I was first in line when the ham made its belated entrance.

As I worked on my paper plate of waffles and third helping of sausage—second of ham—propped upon my knees held tiptoe high, the children had at the gifts under the tree. It was now almost ten in the morning and they still hadn't opened the presents, but they were quite patient. The adults were the worse for it (kids getting up at 3, 4 and then 5 A.M. to see if it was time to open the presents yet), drinking ridiculous amounts of suburban coffee but bearing up fairly well under the strain of holiday good cheer.

My parents had no time for that kind of crap. As soon as the Christmas Eve banquet of liverwurst and schinkenspeck had been laid to waste we were at the presents. As a kid I actually believed Santa arrived while my brother, sister and I waited in the room with Grandma for the required fifteen minutes it took for "Santa" to finish with his shit.

You'd hear a ho-ho-ho and some stomping like Santa walked louder than most regular people. When we were let out of the room the plate of cookies was mostly eaten and the glass of milk empty. The final mystery of the Santa Conspiracy was how my dad was able to down that glass of milk. He hated the stuff and if he'd been born in a different time might have been a major supporter of soy-based beverages.

The beautiful children (and they *were*, both of face and nature) took great pleasure in their gifts and by now the breakfast was done (but you could still wander into the kitchen for another sausage or bacon stick) and I was on maybe my fourth full mug of coffee in the past two hours. That, combined with all the fat and sugar, and I'm in an agitated holiday frame of mind.

There was an Italian woman and her husband in the living room looking a bit out of place. They turned out to be in-laws and of no genetic interest, but she was quite funny and I kept picturing them as Marco's or Gina's parents.

The old matriarch was sunk into the sofa. I couldn't really tell her exact form but it was immense under shawls and pillows and black dress and blankets. She had a cane that she playfully whapped her husband with. His father had lost his arm to a drunk one day many years before in Martinez.

"A drunk bit him. He was a miserable man," the Italian matriarch stated. Everyone was listening. She could command the room.

"Huh? A drunk bit him?" I asked, unable to conceive of the idea as I finally grabbed the last apple fritter that kept just sitting there on the coffee table. I could tell no one wanted to reach for it but half the fucking people in the room were eyeing that thing, even Christmas wiped from their minds by the round glistening donut. After a bit I figured fuck it!—let me be known as "that relative none of us knew that ate the last apple fritter."

"He bit 'im," the old husband said. He had gray beard stubble like a lifer doing hard time.

"Bit 'im?" I said, taking this fucking immense bite out of the fritter.

"Wouldn't go and get it checked," the old man said.

"Gangrene," his wife added. "He was a stubborn old mule."

"He said, 'I wish I'd lost the other one. Then I'd be set.' " The husband didn't seem to look at anyone in particular when he spoke.

"Oh, he was an s.o.b." The matriarch waved away the gangrene-impacted father-in-law. "Sweetie, can you get Gramma that donut? The big one over there."

She went for the final cinnabun. Cool. This cool assed old couple; that's what it's all about when you're old and gray, be like these two. They were the classic couple. Twin parts of a single creature. A couple built over the decades. They hardly needed to look at each other most of the time. I bet they have great talks after get-togethers 'cause they're closer to each other than they are to anyone else. This is a cool Christmas.

The award for Best Capturing the Spirit of Christmas went to the woman who upon opening a box containing a Wal-Mart/Target type of T-shirt/blouse burst into tears. She couldn't even choke them back and it appeared she was really trying. She held up the shirt for all the room to see. It was decorated around the neck by roses. Nothing special but the woman began to well up again and she sighed and "tsked" and "ohhed" like her heart was broken down with joy and said, "This is the best shirt I've ever gotten in my life."

I was truly moved by Christmas at that moment.

Her husband was also very pleased with his present of a Genesis T-shirt. Not the band—the Book of Creation. This one had dates on it: 1410 B.C., 1450 B.C. T-shirt makers have pinpointed the times and everything. He pulled it on over his "Jesus Is *My* Hero" shirt.

But you can only sit around and load up on so much food. Once again I'd done my best; I believe I've upped my Holiday Freeloading Calorie Total to well over fifty thousand.

We then went to my other cousin-I-didn't-know's place who also seemed to rely a lot on Jesus for strength and support and forgiveness. Apparently Jesus isn't much of a mechanic around the holidays because my cousin's rather long driveway had three cars propped up on jacks and blocks in various states of repair/decay. One of them belonged to the pastor. He drove a Plymouth Barracuda that needed new rings.

So we sat on some new chairs in a new living room and a new set of sweet fresh-faced kids (they were all so well-behaved and seemed quite happy. It was Christmas) were playing with their gifts, their Barbies and Barbie outfits, and the missus showed us all a framed embroidery about homes and Jesus.

Jesus! I'm thinking. I've had about all of the Lord I can take in one day even if it is Christmas and then it was off to people who didn't give a rat's ass about religion or any of its major players. It was to the North County Girl and her friends' place up in the North County woods. She's rented *My Best Friend's Wedding* and I feel the noose tighten as we wind up that hill deep into an insanely thick forest. But I don't know why I call it a noose because it felt good. It felt good that Christmas night to be driving up the winding forested roads with her in the car beside me. She was happy and excited that night saying more than once,

"Isn't this so romantic?"

The house is propped on the side of the hill and we step in and they've got beautiful china out and a fine cake and coffee and twelve-year single malt scotch. I love it in a wealthy person's house. I sit grandly in the leather chair. I take quickly to comfort well beyond my means. They respect that, the rich. Walk around like you own the place or they don't trust you.

So there's these dogs in the living room and I'm in my last conversation with a group of people I don't know. It's been wearing me down, these holidays, but I'm rallying at the end with my cake, coffee and scotch.

A couple were telling me about their dogs, Boston terriers, newly invented tiny house dogs of the piglet variety, very short shiny fur and little sausage bodies with pug flat faces. They popped out of the vogue of crazy breeding that swept the land back in the days of the Zachary Taylor administration.

As the man explained how Buster Brown had one and even from

back then you could tell by the old photos that the breed has changed I got smacked with a short quick waft of fart funk and I wondered who the fuck's farting, on Christmas Day no less?! I didn't know the people in the room so I had to assume fart denial mode (I mean, it *is* Christmas), looking as nonchalant as I possibly could, breathing quickly and shallowly through my now mostly closed mouth.

When the smell was gone I was able to risk another bite of the delicious chocolate cake and another sip of fine coffee from the fine china. These North County people fucking rock with their coffee service I decide and the woman is now telling me about a free whelp movement that is catching on amongst some cutting edge Boston terrier fanciers. It seems their noggins are so bobbin-head toy over-sized, that natural birth is something of a trick so most of the pups are delivered by tiny doggy cesarean.

Whap!

I'm smacked with another fart wave and at the same time I catch a glimpse of the tail end of one of the dogs rounding the chair I sat in. I can't be sure, but I'm thinking maybe it was the little dog, the Boston terrier.

The man began to go on about some boring AKA coloration guidelines while I eye the dogs suspiciously. That one terrier's looking at me a little guiltily, I think, and then disappears behind the hostess's chair.

"Oh." The hostess began to wave her hand before her nose. "I think Roxie just farted again. She always runs away. Isn't that funny?"

It *was* that guilty-looking dog! And it's not funny one bit! They're working out some sort of vicious Christmas dog flatulence. That's no good. Runnin' around all hyper, jumpin' up on your knees, laying silent farts all around. "Merry Christmas, asshole" seems to be their holiday greeting and here I am just trying to enjoy the spectacular cake. This affront to my tender sensibilities justified another stiff pour of the Oban.

"Why didn't they breed out the farting?" I asked as I splashed some water in about four ounces of single malt and took a sip. Mmmm, peaty.

"Hmm?" the man asked, as taken aback by my question as I was by the farts.

"The farting," I repeated. "Couldn't they have gotten rid of that?"

"Mmmm . . ."

"It can't be any harder than mashing up their faces must have been."

"I think it's because they ate the other dog's food," the woman answered.

"Yeah, I think so," her man agreed.

I remain unconvinced (yeah, blame the food) but don't press the point and they leave after a couple more doggy farts. The dogs were their children and pampered to the utmost, farting or not. The bitch left the house on a silken pillow and fringed blanket.

So we watched the movie and I'm making an obvious dent in that bottle of Oban (it's not Macallan, but beggars can't be choosers) and the Highland malt has me thinking that way more is happening in the North County Girl's mind than in my own. I alternate between warm squishy feelings and miserableness. Is she Julia Roberts or Cameron Diaz? I wonder, wishing there was one more slice of cake.

She's marking how we met, how long we've been together down to the day and I don't know what to do. I just don't know what to do, but in her room later—after she almost gets us lost up on that hill thick with night's darkness and gigantic redwoods—she's breaking out lingerie (she doesn't give up) and under the sheets in a silky pale peach teddy within seconds she feels just right and all is right and we have amazing sex again and . . . I don't know.

ruined for love

She's sweet as can be this North County Girl and she seems to genuinely like me which makes me suspicious but can I let a Groucho Marx joke guide my life . . . ?

My mind drifts sometimes and I don't know if it's her or if it's me. If she's just not quite the one (but she so surpasses the last parade of misfits for me—knowing full well the great depth of my own misfittedness—how can I question?!) am I cursed with a discontent that runs deep and basic to my nature?

I begin to get hot around the collar under the sheets now with the North County Girl, and not a good heat. Not a hot heat of sex lust that has been my all this past year, but one of guilt that I'm bound to hurt her. That I'm a selfish lout and not even a very good one. What's the point of being a scoundrel if you're just going to feel guilty about it anyway?

A trapped feeling comes to me sometimes in the night. I know it's an improvement over the bitter-teared loneliness that came before, but it makes me wonder. Could one be ruined for Love? Could you become, somehow, inoculated, inured against the possibility of being stricken?

Sometimes I suspected that maybe I'd been vaccinated by . . . Karen (Grrr . . . GRRRR!). That she slipped into Love's potion some antibody rendering me beholden to her and her alone when it came to Love.

Pussy or Love, I couldn't separate. I couldn't distinguish, couldn't trace the trail back to one or the other anymore, not that I ever could. They were one and the same and completely different and mutually exclusive and indispensable to each other all at the same time.

I lay there in the dark, in the silence, in the North County Girl's room thinking, thinking of . . . Karen. She was different from the others. I could sit miles and days away from Karen, an endless smile on my face, my mind numbed with love's sweet drug. Love coursed through my mind alongside the happiness reveries, a stupid grin pasted on my face. It was etherlike, this ethereal love of a woman so amazing, so wonderful as to be impossible.

But where had that left me? Where had head over heels left me? I don't fucking know. No wonder I was so fucked up on the matter.

As the North County Girl lay there dead silent—when she paused between breaths it seemed to create a slight vacuum in the entire bedroom—I groped for the words like I was reaching for the correct change in too tight pants with too cold hands.

She was lying there silently asleep, drawing me to her in her slumbering comfort. It would catch my breath, and my response was to resist. It's hard to fall. It's a scary thing. You're only setting yourself up, sticking your neck out, but here she was asleep. She'd never know and so for the first time since Karen, I lean into this new girl and snuggle against the amazing fresh bread warmth rising off her body. I'm intoxicated as she nestles closer, sure as can be, so I say it as though trying on a new pair of pants you aren't quite sure about. I whisper into her ear,

"I love you." There, I've said it, are you happy?

"Mmmm," she murmurs in her sleep, and nuzzles in even closer.

"You're so sweet," I say, but she doesn't stir.

"I love you." I repeat the whisper softly right into her ear and again this cuts into her dreamworld and she speaks, which terrorizes me.

"I love you too," she says as though we all knew. Everyone knows that. I feel as though I've been caught. I've been busted loving. I thought she was asleep and now I'm guilty of a flash of true love.

She emits more of sleep's reassuring sounds that try to explain to me how beautiful and wonderful and simple life can be with love and I lie there awake and wondering.

e-mail

Subject:
   I don't fucking have one!
Date:
   Tues., 30 Dec 1997 16:52:38 +0100
From:
   macilvie@antik-fryc.cz

I am seeking advice, my friend. Am I a sick kiddie raper? I don't know. I recently had a holiday, the details of which I will now recount, and it may give you some insight into my recent insights. Two weeks ago we had a one week holiday. Mi chica was out of town, so I cut loose. Friday night—normal excessive drinking. Saturday night—I had six beers and was heading to a pub with some friends. In my drunkenness I ripped off a piece of a metal railing (do not ask me where I summoned the strength for this) and was banging shit. I knocked a sign over in front of a shop, noticed a girl in the shop that saw me and took off running. When I stopped, a man got out of a truck and grabbed me (I had thrown my metal railing away) and started yelling at me in Czech. I told him I didn't understand. He asked me how that was possible. I told him I was American.

Then he head butted me, busting my nose open, blood all down my face. After, I proceed to drink nine more beers and woke up the next day with a hangover from hell and swollen nose.

Not bad for two days into the holiday. Then on Tuesday I was walking back from this country bar to another bar and a white car almost hit me. I flipped them off and yelled some shit at them. Later, my little lady shows up and says, "Do you remember that white car?" "No." "That white car outside." "I don't know what the fuck you're talking about." "It almost hit you." "Oooh, yeah. Those fuckers." "That was me and my mother." Good one, Mike.

Then Wednesday to Friday went down to Budjejovice and went to the Budvar brewery and basically continued my binge, but did not get into any excessive trouble, i.e., no monumental behavioral mistakes.

So, in summation, between these blurred booboos and my family's rejection of me ('cause I told my mother mi chica is 17), I have become lost. My one real frustration is the ease with which my family members disown each other. Whatever happened to love?

So . . . dude . . . late, M.

chapter eleven

Marco popped the cork out of a bottle of La Grande Dame in that effortless elegance that came second nature to him. Though we were ringing in the New Year it was a sad moment indeed. Marco's Trattoria was closing. It was our last night. Gina had seemed angry the whole night but I assumed it was the usual lack of business or the mystery man I'd seen the week before or the difficult preparations she was fretting over on this great holiday night.

Marco didn't tell anyone until the end of the night. After the last plate went out. If I remember correctly it was a saffron risotto with fat scallops and chanterelle mushrooms Dave had delivered.

In the end we were all in the dining room, sitting around the table. The entire crew was there: Maxie, Niko, Ramona. There were even balloons floating on the ceiling, little ribbon tails hanging toward the floor. Some of the true regulars who loved Gina's food and Marco's style were there to this bittersweet end, all of us caught up in a sad nostalgia for a time just ended.

"We are closed," Marco announced. He'd been making merry with some old Chianti classicos the entire night. "We"—he smacked his chest and filled fine champagne flutes with the bubbling wine—"are no more."

I wasn't sure of it all yet and sat down with the glass of wine as Marco opened up the small metal box in front of him.

"So let's see, what do we owe Carlo?"

"What's going on, Marco?" I asked.

"Oh no. I knew it," Niko said in that deep voice of doom she sometimes had, shaking her head. "Oh, Jesus . . ."

"Hmmm." As he began to count off twenties, Marco had that great look of his he'd always get when he was being generous or things were breaking big. Marco could ride a good feeling like almost nobody else, even on a night like tonight when he was officially closing Marco's Trattoria.

He handed me a stack. It seemed too big. I took a drink of wine and began to count.

"Yes, this restaurant, this place?!" Marco patted me hard on the thigh. "Maxie, venga aquí, compañero."

Marco could bust out Spanish and Maxie did his usual: pretend to hear nothing on the first call and then look up and come quickly over on the second. Niko and I just looked at each other still dumbfounded.

Marco produced a bottle of expensive añejo tequila from under the table.

"What are *you* doin' with tequila?" I asked

"What do you think? I only talk to you of the workers here?"

He gave Maxie the bottle, explaining it was a gift. That he was a good man, but I'm sorry, it's over; here's your pay for the week and that's it. That Maxie should take a seat, have some champagne, clean it all up one last time and shut it all down. Take any food he could carry in one trip and thank you.

Rock'n'Rollero walked by heading toward the changing room like he had somewhere better to be.

"Larry," Marco called out. "Sit down, have a glass of champagne, have a bowl of pasta. This is our last night together."

A big bowl of the trenette with pesto sat on the table and Marco had spent the day in the kitchen making a Torta Pasquale famous from the narrow steep cobblestoned streets of his Genova. It was eighteen inches across and Marco lamented its smallness.

"In Italy, in Genova," Marco said. He held his arms out like the man who caught the world-record muskellunge (my all-time great fish name award winner) and then had a faraway look. "I think I'm going back. . . ."

Marco then looked so directly at me that I didn't know if I should tell him about Gina and what I saw. I wondered if this was about Gina and what I saw. I knew they weren't doing well financially, but ultimately the slings and arrows of commerce could only wound Marco so deep. It was matters of the heart he ultimately fed on.

I only managed an "I'm sorry. I'm sorry it didn't work out. That's fucked up."

"Mmmm." He nodded and then seemed bitter. "Ahhh . . ." He waved it off and told me excitedly, "Oh, wait! I have a fine old Barolo you'll just love!" and he got up and it was again a fine fun party.

I'd been witness to another restaurant wake. It had that same party-sad atmosphere, a celebratory wake ending on a grand final note because of the wines and beers. Restaurant closings seem to climax with the consumption of the entire stock of wines and beer and the feasts are always big.

That other time this restaurant I worked at closed its doors and an era, a working social world for thirty people came to an end on the exact same day. On New Year's Eve. The night someone puked into the washing machine.

That New Year came in nasty and drunk. A hellish rain broke

late that night, well after midnight. Customers were passing out in the very streets. I made a drunken coq au vin in an electric oven with a handful of potatoes, a chicken and half a bottle of red wine (some of the final booty from the restaurant that was no more) that I had to insist on.

The restaurant, let's call it Saxon's, had been a landmark for some local drunks for the last quarter century. They never ate our food, maybe a crappy app, but they drank at the bar, a rare huge hard liquor bar just south of campus.

The owner, with his assistant Dave, had already collected at a last call at 1 A.M. all his rare cognacs and scotch and bourbon and locked them up in the wine room with an extra new padlock on the outside. He bade a fare-thee-well to the chef, a buddy of mine from way back.

When the last honorary plate went out (I nearly had a tear in my eye, I'd be a liar to deny it) the kitchen crew felt a great pride. We knew we'd put up a great plate every now and then and we offered the waiters anything they wanted and the waiters offered us any drink we wanted and the Mexicans worked the backgrounds. Once we headed out to the bar to have at it, the kitchen officially became Mexico and the dish crew would change the radio and the accordion music began.

At one point I came back from the bar where we were all partying.

An entire family'd be mopping and washing and cleaning (you'd have to tiptoe over the wet floors). Emilio or Salvador would be there. Or was it Ambrosio that night? With his sweet wife who out of great respect for my love of them and, I hoped, my camerones en pipian, had made me banana leaf tamales one day.

"Ohh, como esta, amigo?" Ambrosio looked at me that last night with that look of fun and shame he'd have when Whitey got a little buzzed. He had me with his proclaimed Catholic purity.

"Ahh." I nodded at him, smiling happily for in Spanish I was Carlos, a different person.

"Muy borracho?" He made the international glug-glug sign; his wife smiled.

"No, no muy borracho," I protested. "Solo un poco." I wanted a scoop of that lavender ice cream I'd made that last New Year's Eve night. I hoped there was still one last spoonful for my Vieuve Cliquot. Chef was out at the bar, we were having a wonderful time. New Year's had taken place and I was with my girl. Karen. This was long before she became The Monster . . . She.

(**AIYEEEH!!! AIYeeeh!** . . . It screams but there's something mute, distant, newsreelish silly and old about it all tonight.)

It was one of our five or six perfect moments, that New Year's Eve with the restaurant closing but our love and dreams for self-fulfillment strong and confident. I even gave her a kiss that said "Love." She understood me and said "Love" with a kiss right back. The North County Girl and I never kiss like that. Like the whole world might be falling apart save for this kiss.

I was back. Back to where I really was. Marco sitting in a warm light. I had a pocketful of cash and now a full glass of fine Barolo and great food in front of me. Gina had sat down at the table and she and Niko and Marco reminisced, remembering all the crazy things, all the dreams of food and success, and laughing over all that had happened during the sadly short reign of Marco's Trattoria.

But whether good nights or sad nights or nights nondescript or nights monumental, all nights must come to an end and I finally took my leave. I had a girl to go see. It was New Year's Eve. They like to do something special on that night and I was glad to oblige. I was beginning to shed my scoundrel skin. I was beginning to warm to the idea of it all.

Marco gave me a sixer and some Torta Pasquale to go and I

headed out the door sad and restored and wondering what next. I felt as free as I had for a long, long time as the door to Marco's Trattoria closed behind me.

My mind juggled the possibilities: The North County Girl or Veracruz or Prague? One minute the thought of leaving that very night! was intoxicating. I became heady with the thought of taking a trip and then the very next instant I simply couldn't wait to see her. I remained drunk with lust yet my heart ached for love and with the North County Girl it was all so fleeting.

I don't know. It's hard to say on a New Year's Eve on your way to see a girl, your pocket full of money, no more job. It's hard to know what to do, but I felt great nonetheless. Thinking about girls. Thinking about faraway places. I was full of hopes and dreams, excited by the opportunity and invigorated by the bewilderment of choice, wondering how long the money might last.